FRIENDS
AND
RELATIONS

RECALLING DISREMEMBERED HISTORY

Alvin Cummins

cc|p

Caribbean Chapters Publishing

ISBN: 978-167-3147-05-6 (paperback)

Dedication

This book is dedicated to:
The Queen Elizabeth Hospital in Barbados and its
excellent staff, especially Drs. Allan Smith and Chrissy
Powlett who made the preliminary diagnosis of my
Lymphoma, and Dr. Therese Laurent of the Hematology
Clinic who provided me with advice and support;
Dr. Afshan Azam of the Malvern Medical Clinic in Toronto
who assessed my condition and who kindly referred my
case to Dr. Kevin Imrie of Sunnybrook Hospital and the
Odette Cancer Centre who then accepted me into his
care and showed concern and dedication in this care; the
competent and efficient staff at Sunnybrook whose service
is second to none among the many medical facilities in
various parts of the world (Barbados, Jamaica, New York,
Qatar and Canada) where I worked over the fifty plus
years that I have been associated with medicine.
It is further dedicated to the numerous persons who give
freely of their time in so many ways worldwide, and raise
funds for research and development and in so many other
forms towards Cancer treatment and care.

To all of you, thanks for giving me back my life.
On behalf of those who have not survived, you tried,
but in the end death is inevitable,
but death is not to be feared.
It comes to all.

Author's Note

Many years ago on a balmy afternoon in Toronto, the warming breeze offered a respite from the earlier chilly, foggy morning. It was a promise of another beautiful day in this awakening city, a city that was beginning to find itself, beginning to grow, beginning to becoming important.

I took a stroll along Yonge Street between College and Wellesley, passing through the campus of the University of Toronto, skirting the environs of Queen's Park, the brownstone citadel of the Provincial Legislature, and continued westward into the suburbs, past the University of Toronto—where Drs. Banting and Best pioneer the research into the study of diabetes and the role of insulin in its diagnosis and alleviation, where the use of the Electron Microscope was pioneered, a pillar of the academic legacy of Canada and Canadians—peeping into the glass-fronted shops. No hurry, just curiosity. Yonge Street in this era and area offered diversity. Part of this diversity was these small stores. Scotsmen could enter the shop that offered information on tartans and their plaids as well as the opportunity to learn about the history of the tartan that they wanted to buy, depending on their heritage; or you could do as I did, enter the door of one of the many small second-hand bookstores offering any number of titles—books, magazines, pamphlets—on any number of subjects.

As I browsed through these books, neatly organized by the single occupant behind an ancient cash register, my attention was attracted to a small section with books dealing with Native Indians. That was my undoing. I began to read through a dusty paperback. As I read its contents I realized that I had to have it. I bought it immediately.

The title Bury My Heart At Wounded Knee held my attention. Was fate guiding me? The subtitle indicated that it was "An Indian History of the American West". It was written by an indian, and as the New York Times critic had written, it was "original, remarkable," and finally "heartbreaking and impossible to put down." Indeed I could not put it down, and it brought tears to my eyes as I read more of it.

The profound effect of that book on my psyche is one of he reasons Friends and Relations was written.

When Bury My Heart at Wounded Knee was published, twenty years after the hundred year anniversary of the December 29th 1890 events on that little hill, the wrongs still have not been righted. Because these wrongs still have not been righted, in fact some of them have worsened and in many instances have been un-remembered, I felt compelled to make some small contribution to bringing the memories back to the forefront.

Historians will be better to fill in dates, but the events

that took place and the psychological trauma still lives on. Some cases of amnesia may be cured by a sudden shock. Hopefully enough memories may be shocked to cause historians to join the fight for the rights of the Native Indians who suffered such tragedies, and Black people who have been subjected to unspeakable atrocities, and a new movement will arise to right those wrongs in whatever way possible.

As Dee Brown said in his book's Introduction "this is not a cheerful book... but by reading it those who do read it will have a clearer understanding of what the American Indian is, by knowing what he was. They may be surprised to hear words of gentle reasonableness coming from the mouths of Indians, stereotyped in the American myth as ruthless savages. They may learn something about their own relationship to the earth from a people who were true conservationists. The Indians knew that life was equated with the earth and its resources, that America was a paradise, and they could not comprehend why the intruders from the east were determined to destroy all that was Indian as well as America itself."

Slavery was part of the larger strategy to depopulate the land to make way for European settlers. As early as 1636 after the Pequot war in which 300 Pequots were massacred, those who remained were sold into slavery and sent to Bermuda. Major slaving ports included Boston, Salem, Mobile and New Orleans. From those ports Indians were shipped to Barbados by the English, Martinique and Guadeloupe by the French and the

Antilles by the Dutch.

Indian slaves were also sent to the Bahamas as the 'breaking grounds' where they might have been transported back to New York or Antigua.

The historical record indicates a perception that Indians did not make good slaves within the American continent. When they weren't shipped far from their home territories they too easily escaped and were given refuge by other Indians if not in their own communities. They died in high numbers on the transatlantic journeys and succumbed easily to European diseases. By 1676 Barbados had banned Indian slavery citing "too bloody and dangerous an inclination to remain here."

In writing The Histories, Herodotus, the 'father of History', in the fifth century BC points out its necessity in preventing the traces of human events from being erased by time, this dis-remembering may be either deliberate because of the odiousness of the events, or to erase the memories for political, economic, or cultural reasons. Time's passage makes it more and more difficult to restore what has been lost.

I have written this book to try to focus on events, traumatic and devastating, of people who have been taken advantage of, wrongs that have not been righted, treaties that have been broken, and a sad period in the history of this planet, continents, and peoples that should never be erased from memory.

The tragedies recounted in these pages, based on the recorded histories of the people concerned, have repercussions for us living today, and for future generations. It is up to us, the present writers, to keep recalling this dis-remembered history, and by keeping it in the public eye and in its consciousness, to stimulate the need for remedies and reparations where necessary.

This is a work of fiction.

Names, characters, businesses, places, events
and incidents are either products of the author's
imagination or used fictitiously.

Any resemblance to actual persons, living or dead, or
actual events or locales, is purely coincidental.

PROLOGUE

Disaster

It was a disaster!! It was shocking and unprecedented. I mean, it had never happened before. It was unexpected, but it happened. The island, and maybe the whole world—because the whole world knows us and respects us—was in shock.

The Party was devastated and people seemed in a daze when the official results were announced, especially when the implications of these results sunk in. Although they fought the good fight, the defeat was greater and more complete than anyone imagined. It was obvious that the people were angry and dissatisfied, but the depth of that anger and resentment were beyond imagination.

I never saw it coming. Yes, I knew we were in serious trouble, but I thought that they—the people—would understand. I thought they would be able to rationalise what I did, the reasons for doing it, and considering the alternatives, think rationally and make a decision based on reason and not emotion.

I was wrong! But because anger is a strong emotion that often blinds and removes all reason, if even temporarily, I can only say that was the cause. There was an absence of reason and a plethora of emotion governing their actions.

I'm glad you were not here to experience it. I'm glad that you were not here to see what happened to all the good advice you gave me, and what a mess I made of it. Although to some extent I don't regret my decision.

Something had to be done.

I acted and everybody paid a price and learnt a lesson, but it was a big price and the effect of the lesson and the price paid are still being felt. But at the same time I wish you were there, because I needed to talk to you and explain everything. Very few people wanted to talk to me at that time.

Even Mildred was angry with me, and she knows me well enough. We had talked enough about what I was going to do, but she seemed to have forgotten that and seemed puzzled by my motivation. We had vehement arguments. You know, we never used to have arguments. But we went to high words; hateful and hurting words that cut and slashed, that left our emotions bleeding on the sidewalk, exposed for everyone to see, which did not help the situation.

Peter understood why I did it. That caused a schism between him and Elaine, although she tried to make things smooth between Mildred and me, but the gulf had grown too wide. The intervention of others with ulterior motives who were able, surprisingly, to influence her made it difficult to separate common sense from vindictiveness on her part. She became the person that all the years together and the love between us kept hidden from us; a person that the crisis brought to the surface.

Sometimes, now I look back on those times, I have a

feeling of self-loathing. That played a big part in some of the things that happened to me, to us, and led me to the depths of depravity that self-consciously increased my hatred of myself, and drove me out of my paradise—my paradise that seemed lost.

Each day I kept being hammered with the accusation that I was too stubborn. Do you think I am too stubborn?

I don't expect you to answer right now. I know it will come to me at the right time. But I want you to know everything, so I am going back to the time I made my decision to let you know everything that has taken place since then.

Quite a lot has happened, some of which will surprise you. I surprised myself at some of the decisions I took and some of the things I did. You may even be ashamed of me sometimes, but in many circumstances I could not do better. I suffered in many ways and even sank to the bottom. I never imagined that I would have sunk to the depths that I did. After all, I had reached the summit.

I had everything—a beautiful and talented wife, the best position in society, and money. I drove and was driven in very expensive cars and I lived in a beautiful home. I was respected and I might even say admired in some quarters, and then I threw it all away in a moment of thoughtlessness, even stubbornness, giving in to a moment when my ego took the ascendancy and I made that momentous decision.

Not that I didn't think about it for long and in solitude, away from everything. It occupied my thoughts during my waking hours and I had nightmares about it. I spent a long time at the bungalow on the east coast, away from the crowd, away from what was taking place on the island.

I didn't have discussion with anyone about the decision. I just decided to do it even though I agonized over the implications. I did not even tell Mildred.

Do you see how badly our relationship had deteriorated? I used to tell her everything. We discussed decisions I had to make, and together we made the decision, not only domestic decisions but even decisions on Government business, even on Cabinet discussions despite the fact that those things are confidential. That's how much I trusted her.

The official vehicle took me to Government House. The meeting with the Governor General was brief. His private secretary took me to him after we spoke briefly when she came into the room where I was waiting.

He stood as I entered and we shook hands. His grip was firm, but there was the expected formality to our brief embrace.

He motioned to me to sit in the chair opposite him.

"Your Excellency," I said to him, "I would like you to prorogue Parliament, and then announce the official date for a General Election."

It was quiet in the room. The whisper of the breeze blowing through the windows was the only sound. He looked at me. Incredulity registered on his face. He did not answer immediately. He understood the implications of what I said, but he asked no questions.

The ticking of the clock seemed louder in the silence. Normally it was not noticeable. He allowed me an inordinate length of time to consider the enormity of what

I had just said. Then he broke the silence.

"Are you sure this is what you want? You understand the implications, of course."

"It is not what I want. There is no other way. I see no logical alternative... although there are alternatives. There always are. But I have thought about it and the alternatives may be much worse."

I paused.

"I am sure there will be repercussions, but I have to put the country first. Personal ambition and considerations cannot take pride of place over the good of all the people."

I said it with sincerity, although it sounded hollow in that room.

The long latticed windows of Government House gave an indication of its age. It was an old building, a symbol of a bygone era but still functional, like the two of us. They were a safety measure in case of a hurricane—necessary, seldom called upon these days, but serving a cooling function daily, keeping the rooms bright and cooled by the breezes coming in from the east. The floors were of old pitch pine, golden yellow and highly polished, and sometimes creaking when walked upon.

The large mahogany desk was so old that its original bright brown colour had taken on the dark brown, almost black of that wood when it becomes really old. There were a few files in the 'Out' tray, and a single one on the 'In' tray.

The Governor General was short, broad-shouldered, with deeply lined features, flashing severe eyes and thin lips; a former policeman who had studied Law. The book shelf along one side of the room was full of these symbols. He had been a magistrate and had been elevated to judge of the Supreme Court, serving with distinction. Being appointed Governor General was his reward after the death, in office, of the Dame.

He had almost finished his work for the day. There were no ceremonial appointments later, so he felt he could relax after the matter with the Prime Minister was finished. This is what he thought when he received the message from his private secretary: "The Prime Minister wants to see you about a pressing and important matter."

The meeting was formal. After the few opening pleasantries the statement by the Prime Minister was surprising and shocking. He was unable to formulate an immediate response. He took several minutes to digest the implications. This was something different altogether. Everything would be in turmoil within the next few hours.

"Are you sure you wish to do this?"

"Yes!"

"Do you mind telling me why you are making this decision now?"

The words came out slowly.

"I recently lost the vote of No Confidence in me in the House. Some of my most trusted ministers voted against me. Even if I handed over the reins to one of the others, I would have to sit with them, eat with them and discuss matters with them. I might not even be appointed to Cabinet after. How could I face the island, and especially the jeers and slurs of the opposition? After the scandals within the Party, with the country still in confusion over

the job-cuts and pay-cuts, I thought it was time to end it all. Frankly, I am tired of the entire political scene: the animosity, the back-stabbing, the in-fighting and the confusion. An election will provide a period of respite and allow the island to settle down. Whatever the result, I am prepared for it and will handle it."

"I will accede to your request," he said it quietly, "but I would like you to call me tomorrow while I take the necessary steps, before I make the announcement."

"I will," I said.

The die was cast. The rest was in the hands of a higher power.

PART 1

CHAPTER 1

Sommers Blades

Sommers Blades was statuesque. She often referred to herself as 'corpulent' and liked to say that she "strike back" because she could trace her ancestry from both sides of the "colour divide"—the white side, her mother's side, but she always referred to herself as Black, her father's side. She wore her hair in dreadlocks to identify with that part of herself that was African.

She was relatively tall, almost six feet, with well-contoured, smooth legs. She had a light brown complexion with deep, dark eyes, beautiful lips and high cheekbones. She had a broad backside, something she always said showed her African side. She was proud of her backside, and her Black side.

When she walked she seemed to be gliding across the road. It was a smooth movement, and when she passed men tended to look back to observe the movement of her backside.

Her smile was ever present, and was there for everyone except her brother Steven. Her nose was not broad, but gave evidence of a mixture of the DNA reflected in her surname, inherited from her grandfather, a red-leg* originating in Coach Hill, deep in St. John. Her grandmother had been kidnapped along with her grandfather, from the 'white side' of the family in Scotland and shipped off as 'indentured servants' to work on the Lascelles Plantation in Barbados. The Lascelles was a family that could trace its ancestry over many generations of English Gentry; very rich generations.

When they reached Barbados he was put to work in the fields, cutting sugar cane alongside the Black slaves brought over from Africa and sold as slaves on the wharf. Her grandmother was put to work in the house to clean the furniture and keep the place tidy under the supervision of a black housekeeper.

When she first came over she was sickly, having suffered physically and emotionally on the long voyage across the ocean. The housekeeper, a kindly, understanding woman, took care of her. She felt sorry for this poor woman who was constantly crying and looking over the cane fields to catch a glimpse of the frail man who was just as pale and sickly as she. He was a man who suffered from the sun, heat, and work that he seemed unable to do. He too benefitted from the kindness of the other cane-cutters who sheltered him from the ill treatment of the overseer, another 'red-leg', who revelled in taking out his frustrations on the workers on the ground. He lorded over them while he sat on his horse, taunting them.

The social stratification which existed in the island at the time was a reflection of that existing in England.

English customs meant that the population reflected these norms and standards. The success of Cromwell's forces resulted in large numbers of Scottish and Irish prisoners being sold as slaves as well as servants to the plantations. Between 1650 and 1655 the island is reported to have received over 12,000 prisoners of war, and the conditions of these were said to have been worse than those of the African slaves.

A three-class social system including the upper class—whites, mostly from old English families—controlled the economic, political, social and religious institutions of the country. The wealth, derived from the sale of sugar, was theirs to control and benefit from. This sugar wealth enabled them along with their family associations and 'good christian background,' to institute and continue the maintenance of a Barbadian aristocracy interacting with the English upper class. It also resulted in the legalization of intermarriages, and the perpetuation of their superior position, socially, by giving their legal offspring sole right to inheritance.

Sexual satisfaction through relations with Black African females resulted in offspring who were never admitted into the father's group and who could inherit neither the property nor the rights to political and religious supremacy. As a result the offspring—mulattos—although socially above the slaves, were not equal to the whites. Any benefits derived were at the whim and fancy of the white father.

This woman and her husband eventually gave birth to

a daughter, Myra, Sommers' mother.

Sommers was a young, maturing woman when Harold first met her, a time when she was cultivating an air of sophistication, or at least attempting to give that impression. She would stand at the entrance to the little chattel house she shared with her brother and parents, silhouetted against the sun shining through the front door, holding a cigarette in the fingers of a slightly crooked arm. There would be no smoke coming from it. She did not like to smoke, but she felt it gave an air of sophistication, so she practiced it.

After a time she gave it up because it was pretensive, and there was never any pretence in her. She was very down-to-earth, and told it like it was. Sam and Myra, her parents, never spoke to her about smoking, although they didn't like it. They knew she would make the right decision, which they considered she had done when she never lit the cigarette.

That is where there was a major difference in her personality to that of her older brother Steven. He was of lighter complexion, closer to Myra's white skin. Sommers was closer to Sam, and thus much darker.

Steven took advantage of the local attitudes that gave more advantages to those of lighter complexion. At that time the closer you were to white the more advantageous was your position in the society. He exploited this 'whiteness' at school to his advantage. He almost always mixed with the white children, and as he grew he became more estranged to the black side of his family.

Whenever they made a trip to nearby St. Andrew,

where Sam's aunts and uncles and other more distant members of the family lived, Stephen would always find an excuse or reason for not going. Even though Sam and Myra were hurt by this attitude, they tolerated it and eventually gave up trying to encourage him to change his outlook on life.

Sommers was the opposite. From infancy and throughout her youth she was affectionate and quiet. She seldom cried, always finding ways to enjoy herself with whatever she had. Whether she was with Myra or Sam she showed this affection and love for each of them. It was part of her nature.

As she grew older this attitude was passed on to the animals she reared and the friends she cultivated. She was friendly with everyone and courteous to all.

Since Steven was her older brother she deferred often to him and his mannerisms. She would often sit quietly in their little chattel house and shed tears when he was cruel to the animals, like the horse that Sam once brought for him—he often beat it unnecessarily. Or when as a teenager or even younger he would catch lizards using a noose he would have made from a stalk of an elephant grass bush. He would slip the noose over the harmless lizard's neck, dangling it from the stalk as the noose tightened around its neck. After he got tired of tormenting it he would simply kill it by dropping a rock on it as it lay on the ground.

Steven got pleasure from hurting the weak and helpless.

Sommers' hurt turned to anger as she matured and got stronger. As a result she often came to their defence—

humans, mostly black children, or animals. She hated the cruel streak that developed in his personality. Both Sam and Myra intervened when the tension between these two children neared the boiling point. They tried constantly to show Steven the examples they felt he should follow, and the character he should develop. Sometimes Sommers and Steven came to blows. Quite often Steven was on the losing end.

The news reached Sam and Myra faster than the wind could bring it.

"Sommers and Steven fighting, and Sommers got he neck lock off, an' it look like she going to kill he."

"Gimme Hawthorne," Sam said quietly to Myra. She had anticipated this and was passing his favourite fighting stick to him before he reached the steps to the front house.

"Take care Sam," she said quietly.

"Of course Myra," he answered. "After all, she is we daughter."

He was halfway down the gap when he saw the two combatants. It looked like everyone from the gap was gathered around them. Sommers had Steven in a headlock from which he could not escape no matter how he struggled. Sommers looked up as Sam approached.

"I going kill he Pa! I going tek he life!" She showed her anger.

"Put he down Sommers." Sam was deadly serious and quiet when he spoke.

"He life ent fuh you to tek. God give he to me an yuh muddah, like he give you, an either He got to tek it, or me or yuh mudder. Not you. Steven is still your brother."

He raised his voice slightly. "Put-he-down!"

"But Pa, he know Miriam is a sensitive chile. An cause she black, he want to tek advantage of she. Steven don't like black people. Miriam just won't let he bring none of his freshness to she, and he want to beat she. I had to intervene."

Steven's struggles were slowing, he seemed almost unconscious.

"Sommers, I say to let he go!" Sam was more emphatic now.

"But Pa...," Sommers continued, still with the headlock on Steven.

Sam struck a fighting pose, his eyes narrowed. He seemed almost like a statue. Suddenly, Hawthorne moved. Two lightning lashes reached Sommers, one on each of her shoulders, between her shoulder and neck.

Steven dropped like a wood dove that had been shot with a lead ball from the gutterperk that he used to shoot them with. That was also part of many things that had been a source of conflict between them. She hated what he used to do to those birds.

She stood at attention, unable to lift either of her two hands.

"Christ, have mercy!! You see DAT?" Clevison turned to his fishing buddy Garfield.

"I see it, but I don't believe it. Whack-Whack, and quick so Sommers cyan move." Garfield was just as incredulous as Clevison.

"Shiiite!" This came from one of the other onlookers.

"Oh RATHOLE!! Oh RATHOLE!!" Rupert the village drunkard exclaimed, pulling at Clevison's shirt. Everybody would buy drinks for Rupert at Casey's Rum Shop even without him asking for them. He didn't have to. He was treated like a pet that everyone knew and liked, even though he was always underfoot. Rupert spoke with a lisp which always resulted in his words being mixed up.

"Sommers dead?" Clevison seemed genuinely worried.

"I see Sam do something so a little while ago. I know he was a good stick-licker, but this is the second time he prove it so to me. De other time was when that champion sticklicker come in from Trinidad saying how he could beat any Bajan sticklicker."

Sam was one of the best. Hawthorne was his fighting stick—a straight piece of guava, harder than any of the other types of wood around—that had taken Sam victoriously through many battles. It was smooth and highly polished. It seemed to act on its own. Sam didn't go anywhere without Hawthorne. That is why he was the champion; he and Hawthorne were one.

This Trinidadian had beaten a few Bajans, but then he came up against Sam.

The morning of the contest everyone in the village came to witness it. The drummers took up their positions on one side of the encirclement made around the combatants and began their rhythmic drumming, with the sound rising in volume as the two men circled each other. The Trinidadian held his stick in front of him as he moved around Sam, who only followed him with his eyes, Hawthorne held lightly in one hand.

As the Trinidadian edged closer and the rhythm of the drumming increased, Sam crouched and brought Hawthorne into the palm of his other hand. The Trinidadian suddenly rushed at him, administering two lashes. Sam parried both shots, made a feint, and Hawthorne struck. Suddenly blood was spurting. Nobody saw the move, but the Trinidadian was hopping all around, blood coming from one of his big toes. Hawthorne took out his big toe nail cleanly.

The fight was over. Blood had been drawn. Nobody ever challenged Sam again.

Sommers had no strength in either hand. She could feel a tingling in them, but she couldn't lift them. Steven was on the ground gasping and coughing for quite a few minutes, then he stumbled up and ran off.

Sam quietly went back up in the direction of the house. Someone ran to call Myra who came down the road with a blanket in her hand.

When she got to Sommers, who looked like she wanted to cry but was trying to hold it back, Myra wrapped the blanket around her pulled her close to her chest, and started back up the gap. About ten minutes after Sam left Sommers got back the feeling in her hands, but it seemed to everyone that it was about half an hour. The feeling came back gradually. When they got home Myra undressed Sommers and put her in a tub with some hot water with Epsom salts dissolved in it. After about ten minutes all the feeling returned to Sommers' hands. Myra dressed her and put her to lie down in the bed and lay beside her, comforting her. She didn't say a word. They stayed like this for a long time as the sun disappeared over the hills behind them. Sommers dozed off.

As the night got darker Myra got up and lit the kerosene lamp with the chimney engraved with the plea 'God Bless Our Home'. The chimney was cleaned every morning with a piece of newspaper. That was Sommers' job.

Myra woke Sommers and led her to the little table in the shed-roof kitchen area. Wordlessly she handed her a cup of hot chocolate and a slice of sweet coconut bread. She pulled another chair to the table and sat across from the young woman, watching her slowly eat. She soon broke the silence.

"Sommers," she said quietly, "you are a young lady. Fighting in the street is not for you, and fighting with your brother is even worse. Sam and myself did not raise you to be a ruffian. You are better than that. And you must never fight with your brother anymore. You are stronger than him."

Tears came to Sommers' eyes.

"I sorry Ma," she said softly.

Myra came around the table to her and held her close.

"I know, Sommers, and I understand. As I told you, you are not to fight with your brother. I know he disgusting, but he is still your brother. The blood running in your veins and Steven's are the same; my blood and Sam's blood, and nothing can't change that. Steven wish it could be different, but he can't do anything about it. You have to make sure you don't grow up like him. He fixed in

28

his ways now and neither Sam nor me can't do anything about it. Sam give up trying, and me too."

The tears flowed down Sommers' cheeks. Myra hugged her close.

"Come, love," she said. "Let's go to bed. You had a rough time today."

She lifted Sommers and with her arms around her, led her to the bed. She lay on the bed with her arms around the young girl's shoulders.

CHAPTER 2

Hawthorne

Nobody saw Sam for two days. After the second day Myra woke Sommers early and gave her breakfast. She had said nothing to Sommers after the first evening about the fight. After Sommers finished eating, Myra came to her and put her arm around her.

"Yuh father want to talk to you," she said, "Go up by the church yard. He going be waiting for you."

"Yes, Ma." Sommers answered quietly. "I sorry bout everything Ma."

Myra pulled her closer. "I know love. I understand, an everything alright. Go along an listen to what yuh father got to say. He love you."

Sommers reached the top of the slope above the church burial ground, in the place reserved for poor whites and blacks, for indentured whites, and white and black slaves, although there was no indication of which ones were white slaves.

Even in death they were segregated. There was also the tomb of a Greek man. They say he was a king or something like that. His name was Paleologus (or something like that), but he was a 'big-up', so he was buried in the 'white people section'.

St. John's church is located at the top of a hill in one of the most beautiful parishes in the country, looking over the Eastern side of the island. It gives a vista of the entire east coast from Pico Tenerife in the North to East Point in the south. The breezes blow constantly, and with the soothing tones of the wind blowing through the different trees it is like a natural orchestra. It is never hot there, and it has an atmosphere of peace. It is a place that provides the correct atmosphere for thoughtful contemplation and discussion.

Sam was seated, looking across the distant shoreline at the waves curling and foaming as they came over the reefs and in to the shore. He seemed to know instinctively that she was near.

"Come and sit near to me, sweetie," he said quietly. He turned his body slightly, and patted to a place next to him on which he had placed a cushion.

Sommers approached hesitantly.

"Good morning Pa. Ma say to come an talk to you. I sorry fuh getting you vex. I really sorry." Her tone of voice was a genuine expression of penitence.

"Morning Sommers. I ent vex. I ent hit you because I was vex wid you. I love you too much to get vex wid you. It is because I love you, an could see the possibility of you getting in serious trouble that I had to stop you. Come let we sit an talk. Come close to me."

He reached out and brought her to his side. A tear

rolled down Sommers' cheek. She sat next to her father. They hugged and she began to cry.

"I din gine to kill he in truth Pa, my head was hot."

"I know dat Sommers, but the truth is you don't know your own strength. You is a strong woman, like yuh muddah, physically an mentally. You is a kind woman, like yuh muddah, but when de blood fly up in you head, yuh does doan think clear at dat point."

He pulled her closer and held her tightly as she sobbed.

"It is time for me to teach you a lot of things, so we gine come here an sit an talk bout life, bout people, bout everyting. We gine discuss you, Sommers Blades. Who you is, an who you want to be, an whatever you want to talk bout. I gine answer all the questions you want to find out about. We gine have a man an woman talk. We gine talk bout love, bout the different types of love, like de love of a parent for they child. Like de love dat make me hit you, the love of my life, to prevent you from getting in trouble for yuh brother, even though that hitting was the worst thing I had to do in this life. It grieve me inside. Dat is why I ent come home fuh two days. Yuh muddah understand. I had was to get de hurt out of me. By de way, how de shoulders?"

"Dey alright Pa." Sommers touched them. "Dey wasn't hurting when you hit dem. Dey was just tingling, an I couldn't move dem. Dey hurt a little when de tingling move way, but after Ma bathe me in de Epsom Salts water dey come back to normal."

"I glad." Sam pulled her tighter. "To be honest I was scared." He sighed. "I know I had to do it right. If I did hit you de wrong place you coulda lost de use of your hands, maybe forever, but I had was to mek you let go dat foolish man. It had to be in de right place. But Hawthorne know better dan me. He does act wid-out my thinking. It like he got a life of he own. Dat is why he always wid me. He does keep me good company. When I coming home at night an got to walk dat long road, we does talk. We does have good conversations. I does put forward my problems and he does give me answers. People might think I talking to myself an going foolish, but I does be talking to Hawthorne, and seem to me like he does answer, cause I does get de answer to my problems, just so."

He reached out to his side and brought the smooth, pinkish length of guava wood and gave it to her.

Sommers touched it, hesitantly at first, and then ran her hand along its length, down to the tip that had touched her shoulders. Now she handled it with reverence. She seemed to feel it get warm, and she seemed to feel comforted. There was a sensation, or so it seemed. She passed it back to him.

Sam gave a low chuckle as he took it back.

"Yuh know Sommers," he said, looking away. A smile played around his lips. "In de old days, when a soldier went into battle and performed well, or when he did chivalrous things, his reward was to be made a knight. And de king would make de soldier or citizen kneel in front of him, an he would tek he sword an touch de person pun each shoulder wid de tip of de sword, and say 'Rise, sir knight.' After dat de person would be a knight, an suppose to get more respect from de people. He would be Sir dis or Sir

33

dat. Even women does get de same type of reward, except they would be Dame dis or Dame dat. I guess yuh could say you get knighted. Not because you was choking yuh bruddah, but because you was ready to stan up for a principle, ready to protect someone you see as weak an being taken advantage of. Dat is you Sommers. You is a woman wid a kind heart, protecting de weak, fighting to defend dem. Yuh got a good, kind heart child. Like yuh muddah. Don't ever be afraid to protect de weak. I see how you does protect even de animals. Dat Sow you got, Nicie, she does bring forth eight or ten piglets each time. An you does tek care of dem so dat we ent got to look fuh nobody to look after dem, an de fowls does keep we in eggs and food. Dey does produce eggs faithfully, an each setting hen does hatch enough chickens to keep give we a constant supply of food. Dese yard fowls faithful. Dey don't stray far from home, an each night dey does perch in de trees right in de backyard."

She turned to her side and brought out the plastic bag she had brought with her.

"I forget to give you this parcel Ma sen fuh you. She say to give you this breakfast."

Sam laughed softly.

"Dat is yuh muddah," he said quietly. "Always thinking bout everything. She know dat I would get hungry once I start to talk, an she know we would got a lot to talk about. I too like dat woman."

Sommers was quiet. She was thinking.

"Pa."

"Yes Sommers."

34

"I was always wondering how you an Ma get together."

"I often wonder dat too, yuh know. She like she did like me from de beginning. When I first went to work pun de plantation, she used to work there. She used to clean out de plantation house an look after de cooking for Mr. Lascelles whenever he come back from England during de winter months. She was a strong woman an used to run de plantation house like it was she own house. I come to de plantation an when I get hire I was to look after de horses, an den was put to work in de potato fields, an den to cut cane. I used to watch she, cause I did like she, but I could only look at she from under de hat I used to wear. She like she did like me too, cause I used to see she looking at me too.

"Another woman name Monica did like me too. She used to talk to me, an sometimes in de hot sun she would bring lemonade to give me. Myra get to de point where she couldn't tek it no more. One day, in de afternoon when everybody did gather in de front of de stables, while I was shoeing a horse, Monica come an bring me a tot wid some lemonade. All of a sudden Myra come marching up. She come straight up to me, lick de tot of lemonade out of my hand, turn to Monica an give she one cuff long-side she head, an knock she down. She point at me an say loud enough for everybody to hear: 'He is mine! Anybody want he got to go through me first'.

"An wid dat she turn and went back in de house, through de back door, an slam de door to de kitchen hard enough to rattle the place. Nuhbody din say a word. I learn my lesson. Monica learn she lesson, an dat was de end of dat. Afterward me an yuh muddah get together, an we been together ever since then. We start getting closer and den living together. Den Steven get born. An den you get born. Nuhbody din mess wid me after dat, man nor woman, cause to be truthful, many men frighten fuh she, cause she din smile much. An anything she tell Mr. Lascelles he would accept without question. She word was law."

Sommers thought about this for a long time. Sam knew she was thinking deeply and didn't interrupt.

"An Pa, how I come to name Sommers? Dat is a unusual name for a girl."

"I know," he answered, a broad smile on his face. "Dat is because you is a unusual chile. First off, when you born you was so pretty I used to watch you in the cradle all the time. Yuh muddah used to have to chase me out the house to go to work. I get all soft and poetic one day an tell Myra how pretty you was 'like a summer morning, when the sun rising over the ocean off South Point'. I decide that I taking you to show the ancestors. I get up early in the morning, before the sun rise up, wrap you in clothes tight tight, an just as I was about to go out through de door, Myra get up. She let me know, in no uncertain terms, that if anything happen to you, it would be 'cat-piss and pepper' in de house for a long time."

He laughed out loudly.

"You think I would'a let anything happen to you? Not in a million years. I would'a dead first. I left de house an walk careful till I get to this spot. I look to the east, out to Africa, an I hold you up to the rising sun. I give thanks for your birth an show de ancestors what a beautiful child they had helped me produce. I turn North too, an show Myra ancestors what a beautiful daughter she produce, an afterward I hold you close to my chest an come back home. An when I tell Myra what I do she did feel good. Both uh we did feel good. An all dis time you sleeping sweet sweet. I tell Myra we gine name you 'Summers'. She say yes dat sound good. Den when we went to baptize you an we tell de clerk what your name was, he miss an spell Summers wrong. He write Sommers instead of Summers."

"Myra say to lef' it so, because Sommers sound different an more sophisticated. An she agree, an dat is how you name Sommers. You ent like it?"

"I like it Pa." She said quietly. "It is a real nice name. That is why I ask you cause it kind of unusual. And some of my friends wanted to know how I get a name like that. I glad you tell me."

A few minutes passed with the two of them in quiet contemplation. Sam broke the silence.

"Sommers, I promised to talk to you about things in life. Well, de first thing to talk bout is your future. You do well in school, but that was in secondary school. It is for you to think bout the future. I want you to learn more. I want you to get as much education as you can, because what you learn an' put in your head will always be there. Once it in your head nobody can't remove it. You can lose your house, or your belongings, but once you got something in your head, it where nobody can't tief it or remove it. So I want you to think bout what you want to do with your own future. We got some money put aside for you. That money come from your own labours, from the chickens and the sheep, an Nicie. When you decide to go to university it will be there for you. Think bout what you want to do."

Sommers was quiet. She was thinking.

"Pa," she said.

"Yes Sommers."

"I love you an Ma, real bad."

"We love you real bad too. But we better get back home fast cause you mother done cooking. And when she done cooking she would want we home while de food hot."

He got up and pulled her up, and with Hawthorne over his shoulder, began to walk home. He was humming a tune as they walked.

Is he trying to sing, or just to make a sound? Sommers wondered to herself.

CHAPTER 3

Aftermath

Harold sat alone in the deserted cemetery among the Royal Palms and other trees. He had cleared many of the dry leaves and withered flowers around the gravestone and around the large stones scattered about on Joe's grave. He had brought a fresh supply of wild flowers and laid them under the headstone.

"Do you remember the last time I spoke to you, I told you I had approached the Governor General and requested him to prorogue parliament and announce a date for general elections? At that time I had not even discussed it with the Cabinet, although I had thought about it for a long time. Maybe I was cowardly and even unfair, but to be truthful I did not really care. I had been seriously and severely hurt by their disloyalty. I wanted to lash out at everyone. When I finally did there was the predictable uproar in the Cabinet room after a period of utter and complete silence."

"Gentlemen," Harold began, "I have visited the Governor General and asked him to prorogue Parliament and announce the date for a general election in three months. The next general election will be held on September 6th."

There was an uncomfortable clearing of throats from some, while others looked at each other incredulously. Harold continued.

"I expect you will clear your desks of unfinished business in your portfolios, and discuss with your permanent secretaries and staff the steps you will necessarily take to provide continuity in governance, as required."

He waited for their reaction.

It didn't take long. The cussing began. The blaming, the swearing and name-calling created bedlam in the room. Each voice became more shrill as the import of the announcement sunk in. Harold let them get rid of the venom inside. It had to be brought out, especially from those who were most against him.

He called for calm. They gradually settled down. His voice was soft and steady as he began to address them.

"I have always acted on principle, and always tried my best. In all my deliberations I have always put the welfare of my country first; what would be best for the people. When you have tried your best, angels cannot do more. Even though this parliament, with the help of some of you, has punished me through your vote of no confidence, treating me like a common criminal, I have nothing to be ashamed of. I was chosen by you to do what I thought was in the best interest of the country, and I have done so. At this important time a few of you came to my defense. I trusted people to understand my motivations. I got up at the last Party Conference and laid out my platform, why I was doing what I was doing, and how. I traced a path for recovery of the economy with the least suffering for the majority of people in the country. I showed that even though the salary cuts would be temporary, the suffering would end and through the issuing of Bonds, the recovery could be achieved over time, and what had been lost at the beginning could be recovered. Who supported me?

"When the case brought by one of those same civil servants went as far as the Privy Council, I had to stand alone until that highest court came back with a decision, showing I was within my rights as Prime Minister to do what I did. Still that was not enough for some of you."

Harold paused. His heart was beating faster, for his ire was rising. His voice rose a few decibels.

"I broke no law and committed no breach of financial rules. There was no breach of the constitution and I was supported in this by the decision of the Privy Council. I violated no codes of conduct.

"What you did was to participate in a political lynching—my own brothers. Something that had never been done before, not even by the white oligarchy, some of whom were no doubt behind in the shadows and part of the machinations. This is something the major opposition party would never have done to their own. You know that all the grounds purported as the reason for dissatisfaction—water outages, illegal drugs, crime, garbage disposal, among others—have been blown out of proportion, and instead of defending the actions of the Party that you are part of and defending me vigorously, because of your personal dislikes you either kept silent, or joined the lynch mob. One of those same white shadows referred to me as an errant school teacher. They all showed their disrespect of me, and you joined them."

By now Harold was shouting. He had no control of his emotions. He had to get it out also.

"The vote of No Confidence in the government, moved by the opposition, failed. However, the vote of No Confidence in the prime minister, me, supported by some of you, succeeded. It was a vote against me, personally. Well, let them support you in the upcoming election."

There was absolute silence. Harold, now calm, picked up his files and pushed back his chair.

"Gentlemen, this meeting is concluded. This Cabinet is dissolved with effect from September 6th, and it is up to you to deal with your constituents."

He left the room.

"My heart was heavy for weeks after, although I might not have given that impression. I sought comfort in the solitude of the bungalow on the East Coast. I knew some of them would be hurt financially, because they had not served long enough to fully qualify for their pensions, but the die was cast. Frankly, I didn't care. The damage had been done.

"The country was in an uproar afterwards. The Party

was in turmoil, and frantic preparations were made for the upcoming elections. The elections were the disaster I told you about. We lost badly. I made preparations for my own resignation as political leader, and began working with my deputy for the smooth functioning of the transition. I knew that even though the Party was badly divided, the rift could and would heal once I had left. So when Peter and Elaine advised me to take time off and return to Canada to recharge my batteries, as they put it, I jumped at the chance.

"I have resigned as Party leader. So I am leaving, Joe. You have been my mentor all my life. You nurtured me and guided me. I listened to your advice and followed your instructions, and reached the heights I attained when you were alive. And even though you have been dead for a while now, I find myself coming here to your grave to talk to you and listen to hear your voice whispering to me through the leaves—those Royal Palm leaves you first taught me about. I am going back up North, so I will not be visiting you for a while. You will be in my heart though, for the lessons you taught me will remain with me for the rest of my life. As I said earlier, I am glad you were not here to witness the disaster."

Harold rose from where he had been sitting on the gravestone covering Joe's grave. He looked up at the lofty Royal Palms with leaves singing in the strong, steady breeze blowing off the Atlantic and over the hills of St. Joseph that seemed to be saying farewell, and slowly walked out of the otherwise silent graveyard.

"Goodbye Joe," he said softly, "I am not sure I will be able to talk with you again. I am going to face the unknown again, but it is more serious at this time. I am facing death, so who knows? We may meet soon again."

Harold turned and walked away. A tear rolled down his cheeks.

Harold walked into the campaign headquarters at the Party's constituency office in St. John. It was a hive of activity. There were a number of people talking on phones, and others were preparing signs to be placed on banners and stakes. The candidate for the election had been chosen, and the preparations were in full swing.

Harold felt a touch of nostalgia. He would not be taking part in the election. He felt obligated, however, to assist the candidate who had been elected to run in his constituency, and to help in whatever way he could to win the seat. It was going to be a close contest.

Although he was liked by many of his constituents, there was general anger at the methods he had chosen to handle the economic problems of the country. When he entered the campaign office, a young lady came up to him.

"PM," she said boldly and confidently, "I name Sommers Blades. When you was running last election, you come to our house in Coach Hill. Joe bring you and introduce you to my Ma and Pa, Sam and Myra Blades, and then the rest of the family. He tell we to vote fuh you an to listen to what you had to say. You talk to we easy so, an you mek yourself comfortable in de house. An we did feel comfortable wid you. We like what you say an what you was planning did sound alright to we. De whole family an all we friends vote fuh you. We was glad when you win de election. We was happy when you get mek prime minister. Then you call a fresh election. Even though you resign an ent prime minister no longer I gine still call you prime minister, or PM for short. Cause as far as I concern, you is still prime minister. My PM."

Harold remembered her. When Joe introduced him to the family, he was struck by her attractiveness and by the realization that this family of mixed race had become such an important factor in the life of the community. They were well respected, like Joe. Sam and Myra were very influential. They worked hard to get him elected, sponsoring activities within the community to raise funds for his campaign.

Sommers' pronouncement and expression of support, even though he was no longer in the contest, was important for his ego. Sommers had contributed greatly to his election, and he felt grateful to her.

"Thank you Sommers," he said. "I remember you and I am grateful that you are helping in this campaign. We can always use your help."

He was really glad to see her again.

Despite the hard work, the exhausting days campaigning, the disappointment when people you expected to be your supporters told you that they were no longer on your side, and the realization that defeat was staring you in the face, it finally had to be accepted.

It was a disaster. The election resulted in the decimation of the current government. Only two members were re-elected.

CHAPTER 4

A Declaration of War

It was winter. The ice storm had passed and the electricity was off. The light rain that had fallen, drenching the trees, had been frozen by the sudden drop in temperature to below freezing, coating each branch with a layer of ice, causing the overladen branches to break off and bring down the electric cables.

The entire city was suddenly helpless. There was no way for cooking or washing to be done. Those living in high rise apartments had to trudge up all the stairs, some in the dark, because some apartment buildings had no emergency lights or systems. No elevators were working. Workers from the utility company tried to restore service. Over three hundred thousand persons were affected.

The job was overwhelming. Traffic lights were not working, police deployed at the many intersections tried to decrease the number of accidents caused by icy roads and over-anxious and in some cases irresponsible drivers. It took over eight days for service to be restored, some on Christmas Eve night, although in some places two weeks later they were still waiting.

The pain was excruciating and it woke him from a deep sleep. He had to get out of bed to seek respite from it. His chest was hurting and the coughing was constant.

The recliner chair in his living room provided some relief. He was alone. There was no one to help him, no one he could call. It was after two o'clock in the morning. It was freezing outside. The temperature had dropped to minus fifteen degrees Celsius.

The pain abated when he was in the recliner sitting with his chest raised.

He decided to go to the walk-in clinic, but the clinic would be closed for two days because it was the weekend and an approaching holiday, and there was no electricity. His self-diagnosis determined that he was not having a heart attack, but there was no doubt that something was seriously wrong.

The pain gradually subsided and he fell asleep.

Two days later he walked into the clinic. Many people, including families with children, were there all coughing and impatient.

The doctor examined him and determined that while he did not have a serious problem, almost everyone in there, male and female, children and adults, was coughing and showing signs of having influenza. He probably also had flu symptoms, so the doctor ordered a cough syrup.

The pain was worse the following night and he awoke just as abruptly. The cough medicine did not help, but the recliner did. He continued with the cough syrup, hoping that the doctor was right with his diagnosis.

Harold's visit to the clinic the following week was as uneventful. He was able to convince the physician that he should at least have an ECG done. The doctor reluctantly agreed, but advised that if the pain persisted that Harold should take the letter of referral he would give him to the emergency department at the hospital nearby.

Harold had previously decided, because of the severity of the winter weather, to go back home to Barbados to warmer weather and to the care of his sister. She was concerned about him. He decided to advance his trip by a week and return to the warmth of his native land.

This was the first time in many years that he had felt so ill.

He decided to visit Peter and Elaine, originally for a brief while, primarily to spend a period of rest and recovery of his equilibrium after the turbulence of the election. He now wanted to include Christmas celebrations in this enjoyment, in the place where he had spent many pleasurable holiday seasons before. They had been pestering him for months to come and stay with them for a while. They were aware of the turmoil that had developed in his life. After the disappointment of the defeat in the elections and the repercussions, the resulting descent in his personal life had developed into a depression. They felt he should have a vacation and a change of scenery and perspective.

He finally agreed to stay with them initially, then spend time with himself in his own apartment, getting himself back together. They were persistent, he was insistent, but he eventually won out. Consequently he moved into his own apartment early in the autumn, close enough, they thought, that if anything developed he would be within range of their help. As it turned out things took their own turn and nature decided what path had to be followed.

The ice storm intervened, leading to his decision to return to the island. It seemed as though the de-icing of the plane was taking forever. He was anxious to get home.

His sister welcomed him with open arms and he felt better immediately. The cough persisted though. The pain was getting worse and more excruciating at night when he sweated profusely.

He wanted to die. He felt as though he was dying, but he didn't want to leave his sister. He told her this through tears from the floor where he was lying, writhing in pain. She tried to comfort him, but the pain was too intense. There was no respite.

Morning came, but he was not aware of it. He had eventually fallen asleep. When he awoke the sun was high in the heavens and the sound of activity—vehicles, the chirping of birds, and the sound of the jackhammer breaking the asphalt as the water authority workers tried to find the leaking water pipe—reinforced the certainty that he was no longer in Toronto. He was home and planned to go to the Polyclinic. He caught a minibus that took him there, but there were a lot of people waiting, so he went to the emergency department of the hospital instead, just a short distance across the road.

There were more people there.

He was prepared to wait despite the number of people, especially since he no longer had the use of his left hand. There was constant pain and he could no longer lift it. There was apparently nerve damage, for he couldn't close his fist. His hand was numb and there was constant tingling in the fingers.

He knew he was seriously ill.

As he sat in the uncomfortable chair in the waiting area observing the activity in that crowded, noisy place, a man rushed in holding a child with a breathing difficulty, wearing a school uniform and gasping for air. The orderly immediately opened the door giving them access to the department. Asthmatics had special privileges. They were seen immediately. Two policemen and a prison guard, identified by his khaki uniform, came in with a prisoner in handcuffs and leg chains. They too had entry priority. As he looked around two women began arguing about a boyfriend who apparently shared their amorous affections. They began a *cussing out, and people close by edged away from them. The security guard approached them to intervene, but they cooled down immediately although they continued grumbling under their breaths.

Harold's turn came eventually, and he was sent in to be assessed by the nurse. She was quietly efficient as she asked him questions, checked his blood pressure, and filled out the necessary forms. She took him to one of the examining beds behind a screen within the emergency department.

The curtain around the bed had a floral pattern that was the same as all the other curtains around all the other beds in the holding bay. He passed the time by trying to count all the flowers on the right side curtains. He had to repeat the count many times, because he couldn't concentrate.

The doctor pulled aside the curtain and began her examination.

She was short, part Chinese, part African-Jamaican—from her accent—but sure in her movements and questions. After her preliminary examinations she ordered a chest x-ray to be done in the emergency department, and took tubes of blood for laboratory tests. It took a couple of hours for them to order an immediate CT scan*. There was something suspicious in the chest x-ray. It was nearly midnight when the inconclusive results of the CT scan necessitated a repeat. The sun was breaking over the east coast, and the decision was made for Harold to attend the Thoracic Clinic. The sun had already risen when he left the hospital. The scheduled visit to see the specialist would take place the next day.

The swelling in his throat had increased and the coughing persisted.

The specialist and the residents in training spent a long time examining the computer images on the screens. They scheduled an immediate biopsy of the swelling in Harold's neck.

The result, confirmed a number of days after by the result on the sample sent to a consulting service in Miami, was devastating. Non-Hodgkin's Lymphoma; inoperable because the growth was surrounding the blood vessels and nerves in his neck.

Harold was familiar with Hodgkins Lymphoma, and knew its history of finality to patients who had developed it. His undergraduate Chemistry Professor had died of it, and while he was in training as a technologist Harold had to do his blood examinations constantly, since he was attending the same hospital. Chemotherapy would have to be the preferred method of treatment.

The pain was persistent and the medication to control it was somewhat ineffective, and had to be changed. Hallucinations were the result with every dose taken.

Harold had to make a decision—remain home or return to Toronto and seek treatment at one of the best places he knew to get relief. A short discussion with Peter and Elaine sealed the decision. They were willing to accommodate him during whatever period of treatment would occur. They made arrangements for him to see their family doctor who would seek to have him admitted and treated at Sunnybrook Hospital.

The decision to return to Toronto again was made.

CHAPTER 5

The Battle at Sunnybrook Creek

He was back in the city of so many of his dreams. Harold was back among friends who were willing to help in his care.

The petite female Pakistani doctor—recommended by Peter—who examined him and read the medical notes he had brought with him from the Queen Elizabeth Hospital, was as concerned about his condition as those who had examined him at home. He soon got word that he had been accepted by the specialist at Sunnybrook for examination and treatment.

After examination and a bone marrow biopsy done right in the examining area, the instructions were clear. Should he experience further 'night sweats' and other signs, he was to contact the emergency service and be brought to the hospital immediately.

The emergency ambulance swiftly took him from home to the emergency department. He was admitted within a few hours and the battle at Sunnybrook Creek began.

They made him comfortable when he was admitted

to the room. When the curtains around the bed were pulled aside the view from the window was the side of another building and the roof of another building on that side. From the inside, through the door, was a view of the centrally placed nurse's station. It was peaceful and quiet, and a picture of efficiency. Everybody moved swiftly about their respective tasks.

Almost immediately upon admission, testing began and seemed to continue constantly—blood tests, CT scans, X-rays, insertion of tubes into the blood vessels of his arm that would remain in place throughout the course of his treatment and through which he would obtain nutrients, through which blood would be taken and through which the medications would pass. He called the pole from which the various containers with fluids of many colours hung his 'Christmas tree'.

Various specialists visited and patiently explained the procedures that were to take place and the reasons for them. The first of these, after the insertion of the 'tube' in Harold's arm, was the decision to operate, in the room, to remove fluid that was collecting between the chest wall and the lungs. There was the danger of 'drowning' in his own fluid, or the lung collapsing.

A Chyle leak* had developed and a pump had to be inserted to drain this fluid. It would be operating twenty-four hours a day until the leak had stopped. It became a part of him.

The team entered his room, complete with a portable x-ray machine. They put him in a sitting position, applied a solution which seemed to freeze the area, and began.

He was aware of everything taking place even though he could not see what they were doing. He was told to cough, and then he felt the warmth of the liquid running into the bag resting on his back.

They drained off 1800 cc's of liquid. The pump was attached and it started the process of removing the liquid accumulating in his body.

One morning, a short time after, the surgeon entered and made the announcement.

"Nothing by mouth from now on."

Everything had to enter Harold's body through the tube in his arm. He reconciled himself with the thought that Jesus had fasted forty days and nights, so he should be able to survive this ordeal. Every day he watched the colours of the fluids entering the tube and monitored the amount being pumped out, looking for the signs of improvement in his condition.

The sound of the pump soothed him to sleep, aided of course by the painkillers, for the presence of the plastic tube rubbing the wound from the incision caused unbearable pain at times. Changes could be seen taking place though, the colour and amount of the fluid running through the tubes were changing.

And the testing—blood tests, CT scans and X-rays—continued.

Eventually the colour was normal and the amount stabilized. The Chyle leak had stopped. The pump was removed and the hole in his chest was closed. The anaesthetist was a female physician from Guyana.

He could eat again. Big deal! The food was tasteless.

Chemotherapy treatment began the next day. Everybody was very helpful and professional. They explained everything that was being done and its purpose, except that at that time the information did not stay inside very long. Apart from the weakness of the body, the pain and the preoccupation with the condition physically, the emotional maelstrom resulted in a combination that prevented the assimilation of whatever knowledge was dispensed.

What was clear, though, was that he was in for a long period of treatment with drugs that would destroy much of his immune system. Harold would have to undergo twelve rounds of this treatment.

The outcome of every course of treatment was a period of severe weakness in his body. The loss of a sense of taste and other side effects, some counteracted by other medications, meant a time of severe weakness and inability to do much for himself. It was a period of severe internal battles between the drugs and the cancer cells. It was a war—the Battle at Sunnybrook creek.

Half a league, half a league,
Half a league onward,
All in the valley of Death
Rode the six hundred.
"Forward, the Light Brigade!
"Charge for the guns!" he said:
Into the valley of Death
Rode the six hundred.
(Alfred Lord Tennyson. Charge of the Light Brigade)

The image of those brave men fighting in the Crimean War at Balaclava, charging forward toward the guns on the heights of the valley in the face of imminent, highly possible and probable death, has inspired readers over the many years since it was written. The same bravery was exhibited by the Gladiators who provided entertainment for spectators in the Roman Colosseum, and the 'Kamikaze' Japanese pilots during the Second World War, and must have been exhibited by soldiers during wars and conflicts over the centuries.

Yet today the announcement to an individual that he or she has Cancer seems to elicit a feeling of dread, and a certain inevitability about the end of life. But death is inevitable. Why then be afraid to die?

Soldiers are trained to ignore these things during their training periods, until the thoughts of death and fear are removed from their thought processes. The ordinary man is not so trained, so thoughts of death come to the surface when tragedy strikes.

Religion plays a prominent part in the indoctrination and the choice of what happens to the soul after death, determines the attitude and the approach to death.

When cancer strikes this type of courage is necessary to win the battle, for it is a battle to the death. Emotional, psychological and physical strength are all needed to survive, and survival has to be the ultimate objective.

These thoughts were in Harold's mind constantly during these preliminary days and weeks of his battle to survive. He conscientiously followed every instruction of the medical team. He was determined to live, and to fight to live.

This battle lasted for eight weeks at Sunnybrook, then lasted for many months afterward. As time passed Harold began to understand the extent of the battle and the toll it took on his body. His hair falling out was one of the first external signs of what was going on. Each round of chemotherapy, which resulted in severe weakness, was followed soon after by a series of injections of Neupogen, which they told him rebuilds the blood system.

At first in hospital he was in fear of these injections— daily for six days straight. It was only afterward when they had to be given by visiting nurses to his apartment that he appreciated their worth. Even though they were in microgram amounts, they were so effective that within a couple of days of obtaining them, the body rebuilt the cells lost to the chemotherapy with amazing speed, and strength returned.

As the bodily strength returned, the psychological improvement was evident. He was able to appreciate the need to have people around who cared for him.

Harold, in his reflection, realized that friends and family are crucial, even indispensable to recovery, and to supply the emotional support needed. Every day the thoughts of impending death intruded on his psyche. You are surrounded by those closer to death than you, and those in a more weakened state than you. He thought. Learn to live each day as fully as you can, in a hospital room, with positive thoughts reinforcing the will to recover and live.

The battle continued until one morning the chief surgeon entered and announced that he was discharged.

Further treatments would continue on an outpatient basis. He had beaten the Lymphoma so far.

He breathed a sigh of relief when Hilton's car exited the gates of Sunnybrook, his home for eight weeks. All was well so far.

Every time he went to the clinic for chemotherapy treatments he waited with trepidation for the next visit, and the blood tests that would indicate to the specialists his progress. As time passed and the number of treatments required decreased, it became obvious that the Lymphoma had gone into remission. The twelve rounds were finished and there was no sign of return of the symptoms. The tests showed it.

The battle at Sunnybrook was over. Harold had won, but his condition still had to be subjected to surveillance every six months, through return visits to the clinic for examination and blood tests.

CHAPTER 6

Reminiscences

His recovery was slow, and time seemed to pass by even slower. Time brought back the memories of the election, the intrigue in island politics and what had taken place during the hectic months of the campaign.

His return to the country and rapid rise to the position of Prime Minister he knew had negatively affected many of the hierarchy of the party, and they rejoiced at his fall from grace and power.

His announcement of the election caught the party hierarchy unprepared, and there was lots to be done before the campaign could begin. The selection of candidates, fundraising and the myriad other requirements for mounting an effective platform.

The decision by executives in the Party to sideline him during the campaign left a bitter taste. All things considered, although he welcomed the decision not to participate fully in the campaign effort by speaking at many party members' platforms, he was gratified at the applause he got from the rank and file whenever he took the microphone. He was still popular in certain places and among certain elements of the society, but the subsequent defeat in the elections, especially the extent of the defeat, was debilitating. But the most drastic effect was his disappointment at the developments between himself and Mildred.

He remembered the time he had first seen her that winter's day when she got off the bus at the Bathurst station to take the subway downtown. He remembered her brown fur-topped boots and form-fitting dress, revealed when the chill winter wind blew her coat slightly open. Her beautiful face captivated him, and he decided to ensure that he would meet her again. He was a frequent visitor to the station. He got up the courage one morning, after seeing her many more times, to approach her and introduce himself.

The friendship blossomed after that until they became lovers and eventually husband and wife. The birth of their son was considered, by Harold, to be the culmination of a romantic and heartwarming love affair.

Everything came crashing down with the accidental death of their son. It devastated both Harold and Mildred. For him it resulted in a near descent into depression. Mildred appeared to be stoical about it, but it wasn't until later that he discovered the depth of her psychological wounds.

The eventual offer of the post in Barbados, resulting in his appointment after his acceptance into the fold of the Party and passage through the party mechanisms to the post of Prime Minister and the subsequent schedule of running the country assuaged that hurt—until the defeat in the No-Confidence vote.

It surprised him when he returned home one evening some time after to see the suitcases at the door when he opened it. They were Mildred's suitcases.

"I'm leaving you." She said curtly as he stood open-mouthed and looked querulously at her.

"What?" he said, barely able to get the words out. "Why?"

"I am going to live with Gertrude." She said it matter-of-factly.

"I cannot continue to live this lie any longer. It is tearing me apart. I can no longer give you the love you are looking for, which you deserve, but I can no longer give. I am in love with Gertrude. She is coming to pick me up soon. We are going to be living together."

A cold feeling started in Harold's head and seemed to spread throughout his entire body. All the years of his seemingly happily married life, like his political life, were carried in that cold wave. He couldn't come to terms with the implication.

Mildred was a lesbian.

He knew of Gertrude's reputation. She was not just a lesbian, she was an aggressive lesbian, reputed for her violent outbursts and assaults against her lovers. Was this really what Mildred preferred? Had all his years of tenderness toward her not been what she really desired?

The crunch of tyres on the driveway signalled the approach of a vehicle. Mildred walked past him and stationed herself at the door as he slowly sank into the upholstered sofa in the living room.

He could find no words to say. A maelstrom of thoughts created a tightness across his forehead. A severe headache was developing.

Gertrude opened the door without knocking, stepped inside the doorway, and without a word of greeting, lifted one suitcase in each hand and took them down the steps to her vehicle, an expensive late model SUV.

Mildred looked at him steadily for a brief moment. Her eyes seemed dim to him, but it might have been because of the tears that had begun settling in his.

As Gertrude entered to pick up the last suitcase, Mildred said, gently, it seemed to him, "Goodbye Harold."

And then she was gone, the doors of the vehicle slamming twice and then the tires spreading the gravel as it sped off.

Harold knew nothing more until the sunlight streaming through the high windows of the living room awakened him. Night had come and gone, and he had not been aware of its passage.

He wanted to urinate badly. He almost wet himself when he walked into the bathroom. He rinsed out his mouth and went back to the sofa. He just wanted to lie down. The trauma of the previous evening came back, and he didn't have the energy to do anything. He was hungry, and got up and switched on the coffee percolator.

Reality sunk in.

Mildred was gone forever. He was alone. His world was no more. He now had nothing—no career, no job, no wife, no future.

The house was silent except for the faint sound of the radio in the bedroom that he always had turned on to his favourite jazz station. The clouds darkening the windows signalled approaching showers. The percolating coffee-maker's blue light signalled its readiness. He reached for the cup and took it back to the side table by the sofa, he didn't have the desire to drink though, the need seemed to have passed. He settled on the cushions again.

That day passed into the next. Time passed inexorably, although it seemed to stand still.

He went into the bathroom and was shocked when he saw his mirror image. He was unshaven, his cheeks seemed to have shrunk, his shirt was dirty, and he smelled. He had not showered in three days. He had done nothing in those days. He was a mess.

He realized he had to pull himself together, and the ring of the telephone shook him out of his reverie.

"Hello," he answered softly.

"Harold, it's Peter. "I've been trying to reach you."

"I'm sorry Peter, I must have been sleeping when you called. How are you?"

"I'm fine," Peter replied, "the question is how are You? Elaine and myself are worried about you, especially since we could not get to talk to you. We heard about you and Mildred. Don't ask how we know, you should know that even though we are in Toronto it's the same as if we were back there. Everybody here knows everything about everything back home. Sometimes even before people there know it."

"I'm alright." Harold answered hesitantly.

"Don't give me that," Peter answered. "I know you long enough to know that you are not alright. We know all about you and Mildred from the time you met, and we know how much you love her. Something like this must have an effect on you. Now listen, I have asked my friend, and yours too, Freddie Forde to talk with you. Elaine and I have discussed everything. You have been in our discussions and in our thoughts since the election. Now this thing with you and Mildred has taken place we know how it will affect you. Talk to Freddie, and call us back when you have done this. He will give you some good advice. After that we want you to come here and spend some time with us to get your batteries recharged and get some rest."

"It's alright Peter, I am grateful to you and thanks for your offer, but..."

"I am not accepting any excuses from you," Peter interrupted sharply. "If I have to come there myself and bring you back by force, you know I will do it, and Elaine will agree with me, even help me if necessary. You mean too much to us."

"Alright," Harold said with a sigh. He knew that he had to do it. Peter was a very determined man. Freddie was a good friend, a psychologist with whom he'd had many discussions on a number of topics over the years. He was one whose maturity and guidance had been beneficial to Harold in the past. He could be trusted to give sound advice and counselling.

"I'll call Freddie and make sure you get together with him. I'll call you back next week. Elaine sends her love, she is here bothering me to make sure you come. I don't want to get in any trouble with her so you better follow through."

"Alright," Harold said. "I'll call you."

He hung up the phone. He took a long, hot shower and shaved. He liked what he saw and how he felt when he put on a fresh shirt and a light jacket and walked out of the house.

He went for a walk along the beach in Bay Street, where he had grown up. This connection with the past was necessary to begin the healing process. Peter's call had a significant effect on him.

His visit to a restaurant and the leisurely meal accompanied by a couple of beers fortified him and his well-being. It was well into the night when he began a slow walk back to where he had left his car when he walked on the beach. The neon light advertising 'Harry's, the Nitery', attracted his attention. He had passed there many times and he knew the owner, a former boxer, whom he had assisted a number of times before.

Harry was sitting in his accustomed place, at the door, collecting entry fees from patrons. As he passed Harry called to him.

"HAROLD, COME UP." Harry always spoke loudly.

"I'm just passing," Harold answered.

"Come up," Harry answered. "The show is about to begin. I won't even charge you. Go on up."

Harry's Nitery was a nightclub of sorts. It was located

upstairs of one of the older galleried houses on Bay Street, where Harry sold liquor—without a permit—and held 'floor shows' of sorts for sailors visiting Bridgetown, tourists or any local persons, few in number, whose morals were not necessarily above board. The floor show and entertainment was a subterfuge to attract those interested in procuring a prostitute. The floor show was to introduce patrons to 'Bajan childhood games', like 'Hiddy-Biddy shut up yuh lap tight tight' where naked girls gyrated on seated male patrons to music in a variation of musical chairs, while reaching behind to fondle the penis of whichever one they scrambled to sit on at each break in the music. Each type of game featured naked females.

This was the first time Harold had ever visited this type of establishment. However, instead of being stimulated, he felt revulsion. The 'entertainers' were mere girls. He wondered at their ages, for he immediately thought that these should have been in school. In addition his recent episode with Mildred's departure and its surrounding events seemed to have emasculated him. These bodies held no attraction for him. There was no light in their eyes. At the end of the first 'game', and before the next one—'There's a Brown Girl in the Ling'—began, as soon as the lights dimmed, he got up and went back downstairs, thanking Harry at the door, and breathing the fresh air of the nearby seaside.

He reached his car and slowly drove home.

The telephone was ringing as he entered the front door. It was Freddie Forde. Peter had rung him and he wanted to set up an appointment.

"I'll meet you on Thursday afternoon, if it's alright with you." Harold said.

"No problem," Freddie answered. "It will be good to see you again, it's a long time we have not spoken to each other. We can have a quiet talk and catch up on old times, to be truthful I am glad Peter called me. You know where I live. Pass around by the house. Let's talk there."

"I'll be glad to catch up on old times too. I feel the need to begin to relax. The past little while has been hectic for me." Harold felt relieved talking to him.

"See you Thursday then, around two o'clock," Freddie said and hung up.

Harold took a beer from the refrigerator, turned on the television and sank into the sofa. He saw the beginning of the local news. He didn't see the end. He was asleep.

He was in better spirits as he walked up the steps to Freddie's home. Freddie now lived alone after the death of his wife, and spent his time doing research in Caribbean literature. He was glad to see Harold when he answered the door, and immediately guided him to the patio where he often sat reading and reminiscing. They made small talk as they drank from the drinks Freddie already had on the coffee table. Freddie was doing research into the Caribbeanization or rather the Bajanization of Shakespeare. He believed that if the plays were translated into Nation language, more young people would see the twists and plots in them, and they would be better able to understand the subtlety of the language used to apply the plots to everyday Bajan life, which in reality was no different from that ancient time.

"Let's get to the bottom of your situation," Freddie suddenly blurted out. "I am familiar with what has taken place, and from the beginning let me dissuade you from putting any blame on yourself for anything. Mildred's adoption of her new lifestyle has nothing to do with you directly."

"But..." Harold began, but Freddie cut him short.

"Do you remember the effect the loss of your son had on you?"

"Yes," Harold said.

"Do you remember the effect on Mildred?"

"Yes. It seemed to affect her deeply, but I thought she would have showed more grief, especially at the funeral."

"Well, let me tell you, you can never imagine the psychological effect on her. She was wounded to her soul, to the extent that it changed her personality. She became almost schizophrenic and her other self took over. Her rejection of you is really because she became afraid of showing you love like before, that would lead to the possibility, and strong probability of becoming pregnant again, and living in fear that she might lose the next child. This she could never survive. So rather than take that chance she succumbed to the easy way out, by sacrificing the closeness between the two of you. You are not the cause of her personality change."

Harold was silent. Freddie didn't interrupt his thoughts for a long time. What Freddie said seemed to make sense.

"You know, Freddie," he said, "I have never thought of

it this way. I have been wracking my brains to determine where I might have gone wrong, and developed a guilt complex over it. I need to think of this and rationalize it. It was necessary to speak to you about it, and I am glad Peter called me. Peter and Elaine have been pestering me to return to Toronto to rest and as they say, recharge my batteries. Since Mildred has left I am all alone even though my sister tries to cheer me up. They have been pestering me constantly. I will think about taking them up on their offer. It shouldn't be too difficult to re-establish myself in that city again."

Freddie got up from his chair and turned on his stereo. He was partial to classical music, and chose to turn the volume up on some Chopin Nocturnes. It calmed Harold's racing thoughts. By the time they had finished their drinks, he felt uplifted. Calm had returned to his psyche. The discussion with Freddie had answered a lot of questions.

By the time he walked down the steps to his car, he had made his mind up to call Peter and give him the news. He was returning to Toronto.

CHAPTER 7

Beginning of the End

It was Autumn when he returned to Toronto. The evening sunlight was a brilliant red, reflecting the changing colours of the leaves stretching into cottage country. This aspect of the Canadian landscape was unchanging.

The long walk, even on the express moving sidewalk in the terminal building—a new terminal, part of a new airport—was the first jolt of the changes that had taken place and were still taking place in the country.

The immigration and customs officers reflected these changes. The ethnicities and sexes were different, reflecting the influx of new Canadian citizens and new attitudes.

Peter and Elaine were there to greet him. They engaged him in palaver while he took in the reality of the growth in traffic on the new sixteen lane highway that was only nine lanes previously when he had left to go home. He was glad when they reached the house which was opulent but tastefully decorated by Elaine. It had to be her. Peter always left such things up to her exquisite taste.

They were discrete and did not engage him in much banter after they showed him to his room and left him to make himself comfy. He joined them in the light dinner they had prepared, and shortly after they bid him goodnight with the instruction to relax and sleep well.

Harold slept late. When he came downstairs Peter had already left for the office, and Elaine was preparing breakfast for him. She kissed him lightly on his cheek and insisted that before anything he should "break the air out his stomach", drink his coffee and enjoy his breakfast. Her instruction, which she insisted came from Peter, was that he should do nothing but listen to some music, read the newspapers and rest. He was there to recharge his batteries, not do anything strenuous. They would catch up on old times later. Harold felt comfortable and at home.

Peter and Elaine provided the atmosphere needed to get over the hurt, disappointment and self assessment required at this particular time.

After the battle was over, however temporary or even permanent, Harold felt the need to become active again. As soon as he got the go-ahead from his specialist he resumed his activities at the gym. He needed to regain the strength in his arms, especially the left one whose use he had lost during his battle with his Lymphoma. He realized how debilitating the battle had been and how much weight and muscle tone had been lost during those weeks of inactivity while lying in the hospital bed.

Exercise was the solution, and he returned with pleasure to the activity, camaraderie and socialization the sessions at the gym provided.

His friends there were happy to see him back. Some had come to see him while he was undergoing treatment, and they treated him with the affection he longed for. He soon began to feel like his old self again, although the mirror told him the truth—the battle had taken a lot out of him. His ears seemed to stick out of a head that seemed to have shrunk, but yet seemed too big for his body.

The desire to take it easy and succumb to inactivity might be the reason some cancer survivors take longer to fully recover. Body strength has to be repaired as soon as possible, and he believed that exercise would contribute greatly to both mental stimulation and muscle repair and replacement. All cancer survivors, he thought, should get into the gym after their battle, as soon as possible.

He decided to spread this message to as many people as he could, especially those beginning or finishing their battles.

His return to writing his memoir provided further mental stimulation, and he felt exhilarated whenever he sat in front of the computer and began writing. There was a lot to say. Mildred's loss still permeated his thoughts, but the memories, even though painful sometimes, were becoming more bearable.

He purchased a computer and began writing. As the memories came flooding back, this daily exercise became more cathartic and he felt his mind becoming more stimulated as he became more comfortable with this self-imposed discipline. It became easier each day.

PART 2

CHAPTER 8

Scott's Mission

Harold concluded his negotiations and discussion with the salesman. He had decided on the type of Honda he was going to purchase. Delivery would be made in a couple of days when its preparation for him would be completed.

It was a warm summer evening, one of those days in Toronto when the desire to stay forever gestures seductively, making you forget the harshness of the prior months in the depths of winter, a winter that seems to last interminably so that after a while it seems like you will never be able to feel warm air blowing. Long days and nights of cold and snow so that when it fell it kept the snow plows and sanders, with their flashing blue lights, busy all night, and left snow drifts head-high.

Harold decided to enjoy the warmth of the evening and walk along Bermondsey Road. He had passed there often, but had never walked along it, always driving past. He walked slowly, examining the buildings and looking in the windows of the stores and eateries.

He noticed the sign 'Scott's Mission' stuck into the ground in front of the building. This intrigued him. He had promised himself since his return to Toronto and recovery from the lymphoma that he was going to volunteer his services at one of these organizations. He had seen the good things they did, had benefited from the kindness of those working at Sunnybrook, and felt that he should give back something in return.

He walked across the small strip of grass up to the door, pushed it hesitatingly, and entered the little office.

There was a figure, turned slightly away from the entrance, putting on a pair of surgical gloves, standing next to a male figure whose face was covered with dried blood. There was a small basin with a disinfectant solution giving off a pungent odour. There were cotton swabs.

She finished putting on the gloves, dipped a cotton swab in the disinfectant, and began wiping off the dried blood. Upon hearing the door open she did not look up at first, but out of the side of her mouth she mumbled:

"Please take a seat, I will be with you shortly."

She concentrated on the task before her.

Harold hesitated. The accent was familiar. Its word inflection was unmistakable. It was Bajan. He knew that voice. He knew that body. He knew that person. He looked at the person again. He was sure.

She turned to him. Her mouth fell open. Her eyes widened, surprise showing on her face. She also recognized him. She let out a loud squeal, loud enough to startle the few people around.

"PM!! PM!!"

She dropped the scissors she was holding and rushed into his arms, almost knocking him down. She hugged him tightly.

"PM! PM! I missed you. I heard you were ill and then I could not hear what had happened to you."

"Hello Sommers."

He said it calmly, but he was just as excited as her actions clearly showed. He was glad, and as surprised to see her as she obviously was to see him.

"PM!" She backed away and smiled broadly. "Let me look at you."

Harold said quietly, "Sommers, I am really just as glad to see you. But you have to promise me something. You have to agree to call me Harold."

"Not fuh shite!!" she said, "NOT... FOR... SHITE!!"

"Sommers you mean you have not stopped cussing yet? I am no longer PM. I am just ordinary Harold."

"Not fuh shite, PM!" She was almost laughing. "I work for you during your campaign to get you elected as PM. You win and become PM. From that time you was my PM, an I call you PM. You are still my PM and I am not calling you anything but PM. So get accustomed to that."

"Alright Sommers. I am so glad to see you, and if you want to call me PM go right ahead. You have done so much for me in the past I can't refuse you anything."

"PM we have to talk. Let me finish with this gentleman here. His name is Charlie Deerfoot. He is an Indigenous First Nation Indian, and then we can sit and talk."

She turned back to Charlie.

"Charlie was involved in a slight altercation." She said this matter-of-factly. "Another guy ran into Charlie's fists... many times, until he decided to go another road... away from Charlie, but Charlie suffered some cuts and bruises. I am trying to clean him up." Sommers was laughing under her breath.

Charlie stood and held out his hand to Harold. Harold gripped it and shook it. It was a strong hand, somewhat roughened, indicating that Charlie did manual labour. It was a large hand with callouses on his knuckles and on his palms.

Sommers turned back to Charlie and continued her ministrations.

"Have a seat PM."

She pulled a metal chair from a table and brought it next to her.

"Sit near me. Now that I found you again, I ent letting you go far away from me. At least not without a fight."

Now, after a long time—years—they were together again. He watched as she expertly cleaned the man's face. His bloodied face gradually revealed a person who had suffered from bruises and cuts over time. But it was his eyes that fascinated Harold as their gazes occasionally met. They were eyes that showed defiance and seemed to be burning with resistance. They were the eyes of someone who did not accept defeat whatever the odds. They were the eyes of a strong person. He never flinched when Sommers applied the medication to the cuts, even though it must have burned.

Harold warmed to this stranger. A bond was established subconsciously.

Sommers finished her nursing. She took off her gloves, touched Charlie briefly on his shoulder, and moved away toward an inner room with the soiled bloody materials and basin.

Charlie got up from the chair he was straddling and approached Harold. He was taller and bigger than Harold expected. His shoulders were broad, his waist narrow, and he didn't seem to have an ounce of fat on his body. He held out his hand again.

"If you are a friend of Sommers, you are a friend of mine."

His voice was strong, deep throated, and almost guttural, but it was kindly. The two men shook hands.

"She is someone that everybody who comes into the mission respects and even loves." He smiled.

Harold took Charlie's hand in his, feeling warmth in it. He gripped it in both of his.

"Sommers is pretty special to me too. We go back a long way, although I have not seen her for a long time. We have a lot of memories to catch up on."

"Since she means a lot to you, we will obviously have a lot to talk about... I hope you will have the time for me.'

Sommers came back in the room. There was a broad smile on her lips.

"I see the two of you are getting along well. How lucky can a woman get to have men, two nice men, getting along so well at their first meeting."

She seemed truly happy to see Harold again. She

inserted herself between the two men and put an arm around each of them.

"PM, we have a lot to talk about. And Charlie, I cannot continue having to patch you up. You have to stop getting in these fights."

She turned to Harold.

"PM you will have to help me with this man. He is always getting into fights, saying he has to protect his honour, and then coming back here expecting me to make him well again. It is like he got some demon in him that drives him on."

She turned back to Charlie.

"I am going to have to see Annie soon, and let her know first of all that you are alright, because you know how she worries about you, although you make her weep for you constantly, and then, to introduce her to my PM."

She took Harold's arm and held it close to her body. Harold felt an unusual warmth spread over his body.

"I know you never went to an Indian reservation, so I'm going to take you to one, where Annie lives, and introduce you to her and you can experience what life is like on a reservation. We have a long weekend coming in two weeks, so we will go then. Charlie, you heard me? Make sure you are prepared here so that we can leave early."

Charlie nodded.

"Come you two men, let's go get something to eat. I am buying. I have lots to celebrate today. The weather is fine, the sun's bright, it is a beautiful 'Sommer's day'..."

She let out an unexpected laugh, but Harold understood

the meaning. She had told him long ago how she had gotten her name, so he understood the meaning in her emphasis on the word.

"I have two handsome men with me, and everybody will be envious."

She went to the coat rack, removed her light coat, and handed a short sport coat to Charlie.

"Here, you. I have to report to Annie;" she turned Harold, "Annie is his girlfriend. Her full name is Annie Dream-Catcher. She is as beautiful as her name, and she loves him very much. She lives on the Seneca Reservation, just over the border, near Niagara Falls. Because she can't bear to have to patch him up all the time, she went back home and left the job to me. We have to go see her."

She paused.

"She is going to be real pissed off to see that he has been fighting again."

"You can go without me." Charlie remarked petulantly.

"You are going, and there are no ifs, ands, or buts about it." Sommers was firm and emphatic in her response. "You haven't been to the reservation for a long time and you need to keep in contact with your roots. Never mind you are not a Seneca, you are Native American. Your family is Cherokee and you emphasize this often enough. Soon you won't have to put on any war paint."

She laughed.

"You need to spend some time with Annie and you need some of her love and protection, and even her scolding. It is time we women—the two of us—take you men in hand. When we go there we will give you a good talking to. "

She turned to Harold.

"You too PM. We have a lot to talk about, and you need to see how these indigenous people live. We could learn a lot from them."

She put one arm around Charlie and the other around Harold, and left the Scotts Mission laughing out loudly as they walked across the grass strip in front of the building, skipping like a child with a new found toy.

"I am taking us to Kelsey's where we can get some good food and some beers. "

They walked across the street to the garage of the shopping mall and went up the two flights of stairs leading to the cars. She pressed the button on her key-ring and the lights of her car, a shiny blue late model Toyota Camry, came on. Another button started the engine. Sommers insisted that Harold sit next to her.

She expertly reversed the car and drove out of the parking space and down the ramp onto Eglinton Avenue, heading in an easterly direction. It was a short drive to Kelsey's. Sommers was a careful driver, and even though there was lots of traffic on the road Harold was able to relax, feeling comfortable with her driving. They quickly reached their destination.

Kelsey's was busy. It was beginning to fill with the after-work, evening fans anxious to watch the games on TV. The waitress led them to a table in a quiet corner of the restaurant dining area. Sports memorabilia were scattered throughout the restaurant.

Harold was glad for the choice of seats because the bar area was very noisy, and there was much that he wanted to talk about with Sommers.

He was anxious to hear about Sam and Myra, what had happened to them over the years, to Sommers herself, and everything else that had transpired in his absence. He wanted to know where she lived, how she came to be in Toronto, what she had been doing since he last saw her, and what were her plans for the future. He wanted to know everything about her.

Harold sat next to Sommers, backing the window, which placed Charlie at the end so that he could peek at the sports channel on the wall-mounted 42-inch screen in the next room. The volume was low.

The waitress placed three menus on the table, one for each of them.

"Do you need any drinks?

"I'll have a draft beer," Charlie said.

"Same here," Sommers said.

"I'll have a Molson Canadian," Harold added.

The waitress left, promising to return very shortly to take their orders.

"What do you feel like eating, PM?" Sommers said, after looking at her menu.

Harold carefully perused his menu. Charlie glanced at his menu and said:

"I could eat a horse."

The waitress came back.

"I'll have a steak, well done, with mashed potatoes, and a small garden salad," Charlie said. He pushed his menu aside and turned his attention back to the baseball game.

Sommers ordered a Caesar salad and a cheeseburger

special. Harold ordered a garden salad with Italian dressing and a dish of spaghetti and Italian sausage. The waitress collected the menus and left.

Sommers touched Harold's shoulder. "PM, you have a lot of talking to do. Start talking."

She kept her eyes focused on his face. PM, she thought, has gone through a lot. His face is more lined, his brows more furrowed, and his hair is receding further from his forehead and getting greyer. He is still handsome.

"Where shall I begin?" Harold said.

"Begin at the point where we last saw each other and bring me up to date."

"The last time we saw each other was just before that disaster, the election, when we got beaten so badly."

"We didn't just get beaten badly PM," Sommers interjected. "They burst we ass. Ma and Pa were upset bad, but they were glad that the people in our neighbourhood came out strong for your party, just because of you."

The waitress returned with their orders. Charlie took a long drink of his beer and ordered another. He soon became engrossed with his steak. Sommers reached across Harold's plate and took a piece of his sausage.

"I am your official food taster," she said laughing. "Anybody want to kill you, have to kill me first."

She chuckled and then laughed outright. Harold joined in and they giggled like a couple of teenagers sharing a secret. Time passed quickly and they became engrossed in their meals. The noise from the sports bar increased. The game was exciting.

It was night when they left Kelsey's.

"PM," Sommers said, "I'll take Charlie home. He lives close by. What about you PM, where do you live?"

"I don't live far from here. I live at Eglinton near to Markham."

"Nice." Sommers said. "We are within touching distance of each other, because I live on Flemmingdon Park overlooking the Don Valley Parkway. Providence has taken things in hand and brought us back together."

"I think that is fortunate too." Harold replied.

It took very little time to reach Charlie's apartment building. He quickly exited the car and shook Harold's hand firmly when he got out.

Sommers drove Harold home carefully. With alcohol on her breath she did not wish to attract unwanted attention that might interfere with her arrival at Harold's apartment. She knew the road, so she reached it in a short time and pulled up at his front door.

Before he unbuckled his seat belt she reached across and pulled him to her. She kissed him deeply.

"I love you PM." she said. The lights from the entrance showed the flush on her cheeks. "Now get out of my car before I do what I would like to do."

"You're welcome anytime." Harold replied.

"Oh no you don't," she answered. "We just met up again, so I can't do it now. Besides, I have to go to work tomorrow. Go!"

He exited the car and carefully closed the door. She accelerated and sped off.

As he ascended to his apartment in the elevator,

his thoughts were racing. Thoughts of Sommers and the renewal of their earlier acquaintance and now the possibility of a new relationship were with him when he opened his door.

Memories came flooding back.

CHAPTER 9

Ma and Pa

The ringing of the telephone forced Harold to wake up. He opened his eyes and got up from his bed to answer it. It was Sommers.

"Good morning PM. This is your private food taster. Both of us are still alive so nobody tried to kill you."

"Morning Sommers. Glad to hear you. I thoroughly enjoyed the time we spent together yesterday. It was nice to see you again, and to meet Charlie."

"That's why I called PM. I was glad to see you again, and I'm not going to waste any time. I have to get ready for work now. But I would like to see you this afternoon. I know you have to pick up your car, so I was thinking that you could pass around to the office after you get it. Let's have lunch together. At the same time we can make plans for the visit to Annie at the reservation. We can have lunch, and Charlie can come over this evening. When I finish work we can have drinks. Not at Kelsey's but in a more private setting. Just the two of us. We have a lot to talk about."

"That will be fine Sommers," Harold said. "I'll meet you around a quarter to one. Later."

He replaced the phone in its cradle. He went into the kitchen and prepared a light breakfast—orange juice, toast, a soft boiled egg and tea. He ate at a leisurely pace as he sat at the table in the dining area, just a step away from the kitchen. He thought of the previous evening and about the unfolding of events. It seemed that his path was being directed by a higher power who seemed to be doing things without consulting him. They just happened, but he couldn't help thinking that there seemed to be a designated path over which he had no control.

Why was he directed to choose a car from that dealership? There were other Honda dealerships in the city, or even on the same road. Why did he follow the road to the Scott's Mission? Why did he choose to go there at that time? Why did he meet Sommers again? These were decisions that were made spontaneously. He realized that his destiny was being controlled by a higher power. He had to go along with it, not try to fight it. Destiny was beckoning.

He finished breakfast and washed the dishes. He liked to keep his place clean and tidy and he never went to sleep with unwashed dishes in the sink. He took a shower, dressed carefully and left the apartment.

The bus came soon after he reached the bus stop. It took him to Kennedy Station where the bus and subway came together. Another bus took him to the car dealership.

His car was ready when he walked in. He felt satisfied

when he sat behind the steering wheel. His independence was complete. He had his apartment, now he had his own automobile. He could move around without bothering anyone. Not that he was dissatisfied with the government transportation service, but this was more convenient.

He drove slowly out into the traffic and was soon at the door to the Scott's Mission. As he entered Sommers looked up and broke into a smile as she saw him.

"Have a seat PM," she said, "I'll be with you shortly."

He took a seat against the wall and spent time looking at some of the brochures and advertisements for events advertised on walls around the room.

She soon finished her appointments and came over to him. She kissed him lightly on his cheek.

"I am free now. What's up?"

"I came to show you my new chariot. Fit for a queen."

"Oh really," she said excitedly. "Let's go look at it." She went ahead of him, pulling him.

His car was in the parking lot. She went straight to it. She knew. She walked around it, looking in the windows and even kicking the tyres.

"PM. I love it."

"You don't even know that one is mine."

"You don't have to take me to it PM, I just know. It's calling to me. It's beautiful. Take me to lunch. I want to get the feel of it. I'll get my handbag and let the others know that I will be away for the rest of the afternoon. All my appointments are finished."

She went into the office and returned shortly after. She was excited. He went to the passenger side and held the door open for her.

"Thank you kind sir," she said as she settled in the seat and put on her seat belt.

He pulled out of the parking lot and drove onto the Don Valley Parkway going North. He had nowhere specific in mind to go, deciding to drive until he felt like stopping to eat. The car was worth the money it had cost him. It was a beautiful machine.

It was almost nightfall when he decided to take her back to her apartment. During his afternoon drive he had been bringing her up to date on all that had transpired when they were apart and she was doing likewise.

They were now seated on the balcony of her apartment. The headlamps of the vehicles beneath were being turned on spasmodically. It was not yet nightfall, but dusk was descending. She brought more beers and placed them on the table between them.

"As I was saying PM. When you left home and disappeared I was not able to find out what had become of you. I heard that you were ill and had gone back to Canada, but no one could tell me where."

"I'm sorry Sommers. My decision to leave the country had to be made urgently. It was quite necessary."

"I missed you though, PM."

"I'm here now. You have to bring me up to date. What happened to Sam and Myra?"

"Ma and Pa died soon after you left, after the defeat in the election."

"How did they die?"

"Ma died first. It turned out that she was a bad diabetic

and no one knew. She went into a coma one night. We had to take her to hospital. She died soon after despite efforts to keep her alive."

"I'm sorry to hear that. I didn't know."

"Everyone was shocked. Pa felt it most of all. I went into town to the undertaker and was making arrangements for her funeral. As soon as I got back home he called me."

"Sommers," Sam said, "you know how much I loved your Ma."

"Yes Pa," Sommers replied.

"Well apart from you I ent got nuhbody. I teach you everything I know to teach you. You can tek care of yourself."

"Yes Pa. You teach me good. But I still here, an I love you and will take care of you. I working for a good salary now."

"No Sommers," he said. "You got to look after yourself now. I want you to study some more an get as much learning as you can."

"But Pa I want to be near you."

"No Sommers. I mean it. Now Myra gone there ent nothing more for me here. I going an join Myra."

"What you talking bout Pa?"

"I love you Sommers, but it ent make no sense living widout Myra."

Sommers started to cry, because she felt that he was going off his head because Ma died. She clung to him, but he pushed her aside and said firmly:

"Sommers you is a big woman. You don't need no old man to keep you back. Now go long. I feeling tired, an I ent got no time to argue wid you."

[[chapter break]]

"PM, what he say hurt me real bad, cause I couldn't understand what he was saying."

"Maybe he was just grieving when he said that," Harold said quietly. "I know he loved Myra very deeply. The three of us used to have long conversations."

"I know he loved Ma very deep PM. It was only after what happen next that I really learn how deep it was."

"What happened?"

"I leave home and went back to town to the undertaker to finish the arrangements for Ma funeral, when I get a call to come back home quick. It was the next door neighbour. I hear hollering in the background of the telephone call, I keep asking what happen, but nuhbody won't tell me. They just say to get back home as fast as possible. I had to beg a friend to give me a lift home.

"I jump out of the car even before it come to a full stop, nearly fall down, and see all the neighbours in front the house. I run inside an see Miss Straughn sitting down in the settee crying. Her daughter fanning her with a towel, and she crying too. What happen? I shout out. 'Pa dead!' Miss Straughn daughter say. 'What you mean Pa dead? I was just talking to Pa before I went to town. How you mean he dead?'

"The same time a lump form in my throat, and I couldn't

swallow. I could barely talk. 'Pa can't be dead'. I say. 'Go in the bedroom and see for yourself'. Miss Straughn daughter say, between fresh tears and sobbing.

"PM, my head start hurting me right away. I nearly faint. I turn and went in Pa bedroom. He was lying on the bed. Hawthorne was next to him. He look calm like he was sleeping. But I could see that he was dead. He was not breathing and he was not moving. PM, that lump in my throat, that grief lump, like it move an let out all de water. I start to cry. Pa was gone. But how it happen? PM you mean someone could just die, just so? You mean somebody can make up their mind to just dead, and die just so? You mean to say that because Ma died, Pa just decide that he going dead too, and do it?

"My head was so confused that I nearly collapse in the chair, and another neighbour who hear what was happening, and come over, had to rub me down with some Limacol and give me some smelling salts. It was bare confusion. All of a sudden I ent got no parents. I ent got no family. Steven had died a little while before when he drive off of Hackleton Cliff, and now Ma and Pa dead the same time. It mean I would have to get hold of the undertaker again and arrange for a double funeral.

"PM I tell you no lie, that period was the worst time I ever spend in my life. I din even know how to get hold of you. Hawthorne get buried with Pa."

CHAPTER 10

Sommers' Thesis

"I had to spend time alone before I went back to work. I didn't feel able to do anything. All my friends try to keep me comforted, cause I didn't have a mind to do anything but want to sleep all the time.

"My friend Miriam, the one I nearly kill Steven for, had come to Canada. I talk with her, and when she hear that Ma and Pa was dead, and how, she tell me to come to Toronto. She tell me I could come up here and stay with her while I go to the University to further my studies. I agree that was a good idea. I didn't have to worry bout money, cause Ma and Pa were good savers, and they leave me well off. I had gone to UWI at Cave Hill and get my Bachelor's degree and when I applied to the University of Toronto to do my Masters Degree I got accepted. I sell everything I didn't want, and make arrangements for Miss Straughn to look after the house and the animals. I couldn't get it in my head to get rid of Nicie, but Miss Straughn promise to look after her good. I felt better after that.

"I came up, start school, finish my Masters in Sociology, and working on my Doctorate now, getting experience at the Scott's Mission, and should soon finish my research and my thesis. I will soon be Doctor Sommers Blades, ef you please." She smiled broadly.

"I am happy for you, Sommers," Harold said, "and I will help you as much as I can."

He was proud of her.

"I'm depending on that now we meet up again." Sommers said, embracing him tightly. "I certainly will need your help."

"What is your study about?" Harold asked.

"It's about slavery from three perspectives, by different peoples: White, Black and Indian, who were all slaves at some point, who were also slaveholders, and their interaction with Caribbean people, particularly those from Barbados.

"Our beloved country may have played a leading part in contributing to the introduction or at least furthering the use of Africans as slaves in the development of the American South. It may even have played a part also in the American Civil War, through the influence of the plantation owners who established the institutions in Charleston in South Carolina."

"I know about African Slaves and White slaveholders, Sommers, but I am not familiar with whites in the Caribbean, and especially Barbados, being slaves. As a Bajan I am familiar with them being labelled as indentured servants, but the idea of referring to them as white slaves is foreign to me. And as for Indian slaves that too is foreign to me."

"PM you didn't know that we had Black slaves, white slaves and North American Indian slaves, bought, brought and sold in Barbados?"

He was taken aback by her statement, and showed it.

"Don't look so surprised PM," Sommers said.

"I know about the Caribs and Amerindians were the original inhabitants of the island. But I didn't know about North American Indians as inhabitants of the island in any significant numbers," Harold replied, "And not as slaves or slaveholders. Of course we don't teach or study much North American History unless one majors in History at the university, and very little to nothing in secondary school. White and Indian slavery is hardly ever discussed."

Harold was intrigued that Sommers was so interested in the subject of slavery to the extent she was.

"Ah PM," she said, excitedly, "this is where I got you. You know that you an me are the same?"

"What are you talking about Sommers?" he asked.

"PM, I am no different from you. Apart from being man and woman. You descended from African ancestors and from Black slaves. I descended, partly from white ancestors, who were slaves—Myra's parents—and Sam, from Black Ancestors who were African slaves. PM, all of we is one."

"Sommers," Harold said slowly, "you know that in Barbados the society talks about indentured servants, people who look like you and have European blood running through their veins. They are willing to be referred to as descendants of indentured servants. They will never want to be referred to as descendants of white slaves. All the talk about descendants of slavery is reserved for descendants of Black-African slavery." He sipped his beer slowly.

"PM, that is because people in Barbados and even in other countries, especially those pretending to be white, never want to discuss the possibility and the probability that they might have been close to or related to any kind of slavery, white or otherwise. The thought that there might be white slavery anywhere in their background is odious to them. They want to keep this as a distinction between themselves: whites, and blacks, especially those modern day 'militants' seeking reparations from Britain, reparations for the 'wrongs' perpetrated against Black people, and the success of commerce which profited from their labor. These want to keep it the purview of the Blacks. They seek a kind of purity... Black purity. They don't want to share the suffering that their foreparents went through, wearing it as a type of shield or a badge of honour.

"But the suffering of slavery and slaves is the same whether it is white, black or Indian. No one with a true sense of history, and who is honest, can deny that there were white people who were brought to the island as slaves and subjected to the same conditions as the Africans. They should not deny the historical evidence."

Sommers' eyes shone with a glow of excitement and discovery. She was discussing something about which she was passionate. She continued.

"When I read about the abolitionists and the battle to abolish slavery, they are only talking about the abolition of Black slavery. The slavery of Indians or Afro-Indians in America is not mentioned by writers in the main. And the abolitionists, they make no mention of these groups. The Blacks today advocating reparations and seeking recompense for the suffering of Blacks make no mention of slavery that occurred among persons of mixed races. The Indians who were enslaved by the Spanish from the time when Christopher Columbus took the first Tainos back to Spain from his first voyage, and who were later enslaved by the whites in all parts of the continent, and abroad, suffered equal or worse treatment with their enslavement, as the Africans who were taken from the shores of West Africa and exploited by their white enslavers.

"Slaves revolted against their enslavers, they rebelled against their enslavement, they rebelled against their conditions. They fought wars, not only by themselves, but joined with other groups, tribes and cultures to fight against these wrongs. Many of these rebellions are not referred to in history books, nor referred to in scholarly tomes. Teachers of history do not teach them in their classes, whether these rebellions were successful or not. I am devoting a whole chapter in my thesis to a few of these rebellions. It is very interesting that these rebellions, even wars, are forgotten, purposely or for other reasons. They have been dis-remembered.

"I want people to recall what has been dis-remembered

and   recall that history again, so they will be referenced here."

Sommers was breathing heavily and speaking rapidly. The words just tumbled out.

"In addition," she continued, "this need for reparations is necessary, and will be discussed, but I think the discussion is too narrow, too concentrated on one set of people—African-Americans or African descendants, held as slaves in the West Indies. But what about Africans kept as slaves by Indians? What about Indians kept as slaves by the white man, and who were not only kept in enslavement, but had their land, a whole continent, taken from them? Don't they deserve some considerations and reparations also? What do you think?"

She didn't give him time to reply.

"For instance, slavery, as distinct from slavery involving a specific ethnic group or society, has been accepted as a part of living since time immemorial. The Bible talks about Moses leading the Hebrew slaves out of bondage by Pharaohs, African and Black. The Greek philosopher Aristotle perceived slavery not only as a need to be fulfilled in society, but as a right, of the more 'civilized' societies. Both Christianity and Islam accepted the keeping of slaves as a natural fact of living. Even though Christians rejected the keeping of Christian slaves, they had no objection to heathens, Muslims or people of either, or neither side, being enslaved. This is why when Christopher Columbus offered slaves to Queen Isabella, he was careful to point out that they were idolaters."

Harold stopped her.

"This subject is complicated and we will have to go through it systematically. Let's discuss this further. It's getting late and I really should be going home. Your car is still in the parking garage."

He started to get up. Sommers stopped him.

"PM," she sat on his lap, and put her hands on his shoulders. I was just getting wound up, but I agree with you."

She looked him in his eyes.

"Now PM, let me tell you something. And I am saying this in all seriousness. After tonight I ent taking you home, an' just because you got your car now don't mean that I ent going worry about you when you leave here. I told you at the apartment door that I love you. I meant it. I am here alone, and therefore any time you are here with me you can stay.

"Miriam was my friend and confidante for years, and then she get diagnose with diabetes, like Ma. She had to go pun dialysis. Then she get worse. Next thing I had to bury her too. She leave me in her will, an I inherit everything she had. After that I was all alone. I only had my studies to keep me occupied. Pa and Ma give me the strength to keep pun a steady path.

"You can sleep here with me, and consider this your home. Never mind you have your own apartment. I see no need for either of us to be alone. We can have each other. I know what it is to be alone, not to have someone to cuddle up to, not to have someone next to you when certain parts start to itch. Not to have someone to make love to. I know what it is not to have a shoulder to cry on or someone to share a laugh with. PM, I want you to be that person. I want you to be my man, cause I consider myself your woman."

Harold was silent. He was surprised and touched. Since he and Mildred had separated and she sought the divorce which he did not contest, although he was deeply hurt to the extent that he had withdrawn into himself and had not cultivated any close relationship with any other woman, what Sommers said resonated with him. He too missed that companionship. He was really hurt to discover Mildred's lesbianism and to lose her to a lesbian politician.

Sommers was offering him that element that was missing in his life. He was really attracted to her and wanted her. She was pretty, talented, well educated, and had a kind and understanding nature. She was desirable. Now the opportunity to experience her and rekindle that spark was being offered.

He drew her to him and offered his lips. She kissed him deeply. She moaned as her excitement grew. She hugged him. Her breasts rose in response. She pulled one out and offered it to him.

"PM, these are yours any time and every time you want them. Do you?"

"Yes Sommers. I do," he gasped.

He suckled them. The second breast followed the first. She rose, and holding him by his hand, led him into her bedroom. She pushed him onto the bed, and while he lay there watching her, she began to undress.

"PM," she said as she removed her blouse and bras,

"I'm your private dancer."

Her skirt fell to the floor. She stepped out of it. She was completely naked. She was beautiful.

"Sommers," he said gently in her ear. She was lying beside him, gently rubbing his nipple. "I care deeply for you. I promise to take care of you. I know the love that Sam had for Myra, and I will try and give you that same love. I will always be there for you, and I will try and protect you from any harm that might come your way.'

"PM." Sommers turned and kissed him tenderly. "PM, I am your woman. I will always make you proud of me."

"Sommers," he said, "I'm not going home tonight."

"I had no intention of letting you go home. I make up my mind when you were passing by Newmarket. Not tonight, first of all, and especially after what just took place. You tek everything out of me."

She rolled over and was soon fast asleep. Harold fell asleep soon after. What had just taken place occupied his thoughts.

They ate breakfast together, and then showered together. Harold watched the morning news on television while she readied herself for work. He quickly dropped her off at the Scott's Mission and then went to his apartment. He went grocery shopping because he planned to invite his new friends over for a visit in the near future.

Sommers soon called him to let him know when they were going to see Annie. She and Annie had made the arrangement, and she would come over later in the evening. He offered to prepare a meal for the two of them.

He busied himself around the apartment, washing

his clothes and cleaning up and tidying his work place. He had a tendency to work at his desk and scatter his papers. Sommers' thesis offered an opportunity to get back into the world of research and writing again.

CHAPTER 11

My PM

Sommers arrived at Harold's apartment. She had called earlier and invited herself over for breakfast. He had finished showering and dressing when the buzzer to his apartment indicated that she had arrived.

As soon as he opened the door for her she leaped into his arms, kissing him deeply.

"Good morning, PM. I'm starving, so don't keep a girl waiting."

He had to deter her, since she wanted, as she said, to 'get an eye-opener'.

"That has to wait till later," he said. "I am sure Charlie is waiting for us."

"Well alright," she said with a pout, "but I will regard that as a promise to be fulfilled, very soon."

They finished breakfast and left for Charlie's apartment. When they arrived at the apartment he remained seated in the vehicle while she entered the lobby and pressed the buzzer. Charlie answered on the intercom.

"Hello," he said when she identified herself. "I'll be right down."

He soon joined them.

Sommers maneuvered her car into the steady stream of traffic on the highway. She called Annie's number on her car phone.

"Hello Annie," she said when Annie's voice—with a soft, mellifluous, slightly accented tone—replied.

"Sommers here. I am on my way to the reservation with two lovely men. Mr. Deerfoot whom you know, and Harold, my PM whom you will meet for the first time. We should be there in about two hours."

"All right," Annie replied. "You are all welcome. I will be glad to see Charlie. Looking forward to that."

Traffic was filling all the lanes of the sixteen lane highway, and moving swiftly. They made good progress, not conversing much. Harold was impressed with the progress that had been made on highway improvement during the years he had been away from the country. They were passing through the grape growing district. It was the wine producing country of Ontario. One thing he noted was the advertisements for farmland that. This would have repercussions for the future, he thought.

They were at the border between Canada and the United States well within the estimated time. They quickly passed through American immigration and were on the way to the Seneca Reservation where Annie lived. As they approached the reservation, passing the entrance to the Seneca Casino, a modern complex decorated with native painting and Indian figures, Harold was given a short introduction to the history of the Seneca indigenous people by Sommers.

"Annie will fill you in on the history of this area and of the Seneca tribe. Can you imagine that all this area is part of the territory owned by the Seneca tribe? The Casino and places like that are controlled by them. The Niagara Falls are on lands owned by the Seneca, even today," she said as they passed a complex of small stores and smoke shops.

They reached the entrance to a number of buildings, bungalows, and stores and a number of tepees on a grassy area. Native paintings and a small building advertising native arts and craft were around the entrance to the reservation.

They had arrived and Annie was there to welcome them. She was pretty, with deeply bronzed skin, high cheek bones with a pert nose, and two long plaits of black hair hung from each side of her head, kept in place on her head by a head band festooned with fine coloured beads. She was slender, reaching Harold's shoulder, and wore a dress made of the finest deerskin leather, with tassels around the shoulders and hem of the dress. Coloured beads were sewn in the front and around the arms, and around the deerskin moccasins on her small feet, and the deerskin band around her forehead.

Sommers went up to her and they embraced. Charlie stayed slightly behind them. He seemed embarrassed. Sommers turned to Harold.

"Annie," she said, "This is PM, my PM. His real name is Harold, but I refuse to call him that because we go back a long way. He was formerly Prime Minister of our country.

110

I campaigned for him during his election campaign. He won that election, that's when he became my PM.

"I will tell you the sorry story of why he is no longer prime minister, but that will take a while to tell, so I will keep that for later. It's enough for you to know now that I brought him to meet you, and I am sure when you get to know him better you will find out what a wonderful person he is."

Harold reached out and shook Annie's hand. It was warm and the grip was firm.

"Pleased to meet you Annie. I am sure we will become very good friends."

Annie looked past Sommers.

"And who is this other man with you?" There was a twinkle in her eyes. "I seem to remember him from somewhere. He looks familiar, like someone I knew from the past, but I have not seen him for so long I hardly remember him."

She walked up to Charlie. "Do I know you?"

She reached out and grabbed Charlie by his shirt collar. She pulled him to her and kissed him. Charlie put his arms around her and kissed her back. They embraced for a long time. There were tears in Annie's eyes.

"Sommers," she said, "I remember him now. Thanks for bringing back my lost sheep. I missed him." She turned to Charlie. "Listen buster, if you think you are going to put me through what I have gone through for the recent past, you have another think coming. We have a lot to talk about, so be prepared." Harold liked her voice.

She put her arm around Sommers.

"Come Sommers, you must be tired from the drive. Let's get something to eat and then we will do some talking. I have to learn of this PM of yours. I hope he will not object to me calling him PM also, I sort of like the sound of my PM."

"Now is as good as any to tell you about my PM." Sommers began as she and Annie moved into the kitchen area. [[[kitchen area? I thought they were at the entrance]]]

"This story begins a long time ago, although time has passed so quickly that it seems like yesterday. He walked into the campaign headquarters during the election campaign. Joe, the village cabinet maker, one of the most trusted and respected men in the district, brought him. When Joe gave his word, it was accepted by everyone as a contract. Everyone liked him and respected him. Therefore when he brought this young, handsome man into our household and every other household in the village and asked us to vote for him, we all agreed to support him.

"I was attracted to him right away. I could hardly keep my eyes, or my hands, off him. I was rather precocious in my younger days, but Ma kept a strict eye on me, so I had to behave myself. We worked hard to get him elected. I spent many hours and days walking the hills and roads in the district canvassing for him and the party.

"My PM won the election and was chosen by the other successful party members as Prime Minister. I felt so proud when he led his party into the hallowed chambers of the House of Assembly. Ma, Pa, and myself were special guests at the opening ceremony. We all felt proud of the part we played in getting him elected. After that he was almost like family.

"Then the recession struck. The country fell on hard times and decisive action had to be taken. Civil servants had their salaries cut, people were laid off and there was widespread discontent. The Unions and the private sector organized protest marches. The opposition sponsored a vote of no-confidence in the government. That motion failed, but then they sponsored a vote of no-confidence in the Prime Minister. When the voice vote was taken, some of PM's own cabinet colleagues voted against him. Can you imagine that?"

There was a catch in her throat and tears showed in her eyes.

"Annie, some of his most trusted friends and colleagues sided with the opposition party to bring down my PM."

Annie felt like crying herself.

"I can understand how he must have felt," Annie said quietly, "And I can understand your feelings."

Sommers continued.

"It was at that time that I realized how much I cared for this man." She reached out and put her arms around Harold. "That is why, now that we have met again, I have no intention of letting him get away again. Especially now that he has recovered from the illness that almost took him away for good. So Annie you now know the story of my PM."

"Let's eat," Charlie interrupted. This story has made

me hungry. Especially now that I have met your PM and I realize what he has gone through. These sorts of things make me hungry."

They moved into the dining area.

CHAPTER 12

The Trail of Tears

It was a warm afternoon. They were seated on the grass outside the tepee. The sun had passed its zenith and the breeze blowing across the seemingly endless grassland before them, wheat interspersed with barley stalks seeking the sun, made the atmosphere pleasant. Annie sat across from Charlie, never seeming to take her eyes from his face. His cuts were healing.

Harold sat cross-legged and Sommers was beside him with her head on his lap. It was a peaceful scene.

"PM," Charlie blurted out suddenly. "Sommers wants me to tell you my story."

Charlie continued speaking, not waiting to see who was listening. He knew everybody would want to hear what he had to say. He seemed to be concentrating on some image in the distant sky. His voice was low and the words flowed smoothly as his memory brought back the picture.

"My father and my mother lived with my grandfather in the log cabin that my grandfather had built on the land they owned in Georgia." He paused.

"In Georgia?" Harold asked.

"Yes, way down south in Georgia." Charlie responded.

"How come all the way in Georgia?" Harold said, plucking a piece of grass and chewing on it slowly.

"Because that was our land. We Cherokees, the Creek, the Choctaws, the Seminoles, were five Indian tribes that owned and lived on that land. We once owned all the land of that state." He turned to Harold. "Have you ever heard of the Trail of Tears?"

"Never heard of it."

"I read about it," Sommers said. There was sombreness in her voice.

"That is one of the episodes many of us Indians keep in our hearts. We can never forget." Annie interjected. There was anger in her voice.

"Indians can never forget it, nor should they." Charlie added.

"What was the Trail of Tears?" Harold asked.

"The best way to educate you about that tragedy is to experience it through the words and eyes of my grandfather. The history of the native indians is a history told by them as they related it over the years, repeating the words over and over again. Theirs is an oral history."

[[[chapter break]]]

My father, before he died, told me about our lives. That was before Black Bear became my father. We Cherokee were the ones particularly affected, although other Indian Tribes also walked that trail. We lived with my grandfather and grandmother in the log cabin that my grandfather had built on our land. The farm was their support. He raised cattle, farmed, and kept peach trees that he was really proud of. My grandfather, Braveheart, was a Cherokee warrior and was known for his exploits as a fighter.

They were part of the Cherokee families forcibly removed from their lands and escorted by American soldiers, made to walk from Georgia to Oklahoma, to the 'Indian lands' out West, land that had been designated as Indian lands by the American Government under President Andrew Jackson, who enforced the Indian Removal Act.

Brave Heart's bravery and pride were legendary, and they were brought to the surface when the soldiers came and told them that they had to leave everything and move out West. The soldiers came one morning, a whole squad of them. They approached all the cabins in our area and began breaking doors and forcing the people out with their rifles with bayonets. There was mass confusion. Nobody knew where we were going.

"Out West? But where was out West?" Brave Heart was furious. "We do not know where we are going." He said to the soldier.

"You have to leave," the soldier said.

"Why?" Brave Heart asked.

"Because you have to give up your house and farm and go out west."

"Out west where?"

"I don't know and I don't care," the soldier said.

"Then I am not moving!"

Brave Heart stood at the door and folded his hands. The soldier attempted to push past him. He resisted and

117

the two of them struggled.

More soldiers came, and soon Brave heart was fighting with five of them. Charlie's grandfather became involved. His father was at school. [[[isn't Charlie's grandfather the narrator of this story?]]]

The soldiers beat Brave Heart with their rifles and one of them stabbed him with the bayonet. He fell to the floor bleeding. The soldiers dragged him and Grandfather out of the cabin and pushed them into the wagon. They threw a few of the belongings on the wagon and made it move away with them to join the other members of the tribe undergoing the same treatment.

The soldiers started to ransack the cabin and destroy what they did not want for themselves. His grandfather's wound was attended to by people from another wagon who came to help.

The scene was one of chaos. Grandfather was confused. All the Cherokees were confused. Why did they have to leave the cabins they had built with their own hands, leave the fields they had ploughed? Why did they have to leave and go out west? Had they not adjusted to the way of the white man? Hadn't they given up the way of the Cherokee and become farmers? Hadn't they even begun to keep Africans as slaves because the White man had showed the example by keeping the Africans as slaves, and emphasizing that keeping African slaves was part of the requirement to be a farmer, like the white man?

They were no longer hunters or fighters, fighting against the white man. Hadn't they stopped teaching their sons about the way of the Indian and sent them to the white

118

man's school?

He was a peaceful man now. The way of the Indian was slowly fading. The Cherokee were no longer powerful.

The Indians talked excitedly to each other. They discussed the reasons for their removal. Lone Wolf, leader of the tribe, addressed the people gathered on the wagons.

Brave Heart's bleeding had stopped, but he was weak.

"Gather around, my brothers and sisters. The white man has once more shown that he speaks with a forked tongue," Lone Wolf said.

"The Great White Father in Washington, President Andrew Jackson, who promised that '...As long as the sun shines and the grass grows there would be peace between him and the Indians', he still decided that all Indians east of the Mississippi would have to move to Indian lands out west. This was decreed by the Indian Removal Act."

There was consternation. Nobody knew what was going on. There was excitement among the Cherokees. Everybody was speaking at the same time. Lone Wolf tried to keep order. The soldiers kept order with their bayonets and rifles.

"The land the Indians had lived and hunted on for a thousand years is now to be occupied by white men who want to live on these lands, where gold has recently been discovered," he said. "This gold will not belong to the Indians, the white man will now own it."

Despite the fact that the Indian Removal Act had been

challenged by the Indians in the Supreme court, and the Indians chose the white man's way, believing the white man that this was the 'peaceful' way to go and that they had won the case, Andrew Jackson ignored the result. He showed his contempt for the supreme court of the white man and its laws and decisions, the very law they wanted us to obey. He had instructed that "the Indian had to go."

In spite of the treaties that had been signed between the Indian and the white man, the white man's way had to prevail. The Indians would be removed out West.

When Standing Deer's father came home from school he could not find his parents. The log cabin was burning. It burned to the ground. It took him four days of frantic searching to find his parents. Other children also couldn't find their parents.

There were not enough wagons for everybody. Others had to walk. 6,000 Cherokees in his father's group left. 4,000 died on the journey. The Cherokee Nation never recovered.

Brave Heart died after two weeks. The wagons travelled slowly. The winter was brutal and the people had little food and clothing or clean water. Many suffered from disease and cold. When Brave Heart died he could never forget the look in his eyes as the light slowly left them.

My mother became sicker. Blood came when she coughed. Her skin, what little there was of it, was always hot and left her bones. She became too sick and weak to travel and one day, in the middle of winter, she couldn't.

My father put her to sit in the arms of a young pine tree. The snow began falling slowly. The snowflakes were large. They were sitting there as the wagons disappeared over the horizon. I never saw them again. Black Bear became my parents.

CHAPTER 13

A Horse for a Brave

"Annie, whatever I do, sit as still as you can. Do not move. Do not even blink your eyes. Do not move a muscle. PM and Sommers, do not make any sudden moves, be still."

In a flash his hand moved and disappeared in the grass next to Annie. It emerged holding a rattlesnake in its grasp, holding it behind its head, its body wrapped around his arm, its rattles vibrating loudly. He jumped up with it.

Annie squealed. Sommers jumped. Harold was transfixed. He was afraid of snakes. There were no snakes of that kind in Barbados.

Charlie was talking to the snake.

"You naughty thing," he said, "you know that anybody else would kill you right way. You should not even be around here. You scared Annie. I will not kill you but you must not come around here again."

He walked slowly away from them, about a hundred yards, and uncurling it from around his arm, threw it into the bushes.

Sommers was sweating. She touched the marks on her shoulders. Charlie's sudden movement reminded her of her father and Hawthorne. She started to cry quietly. Harold reached out and hugged her. She clung to him as she kept sobbing.

Charlie came up to Annie.

"I saw it approaching you," he said.

"I never even realized they were still around here." She said quietly.

"The warm day must have brought it out of the hole it would normally be in at this time."

Annie kissed him on his cheek.

"I have something for you," she said. "I was waiting for the right time to give it to you. I'm glad Sommers brought you home now. It's the right time. I bought it for you a while ago, but you wouldn't come back to the reservation so I couldn't give it to you."

She left and went past the tepee to the barn at the back of the bungalow. She came back leading a horse. It was a magnificent animal. Its skin shone, its muscles rippled and it held its head erect as it walked quietly beside her. It was well cared for.

Charlie perked up when he saw it.

"I haven't named him yet. I wanted you to do it."

"Is it really for me?" he asked.

"Of course."

"He is really magnificent."

"You deserve him. Even though you have been naughty again, according to Sommers."

"No I have not." He was defensive.

"Yes you have been. I can see it in your face. Those cuts are fresh."

"I was defending the honour of our tribe and the Indian people."

She was defiant.

"Charlie, you cannot keep fighting like this, you will get yourself killed. Everyone will not resort to fists to settle their differences of opinion."

The stallion neighed softly. Charlie walked all around it. He ran his hand over its chest and down its rump. The horse followed his examination without moving around. It followed him with its eyes and ears.

"See? He likes you." Annie said.

"I like him too." Charlie replied.

Annie handed him the halter and the lead.

"He is yours. Thanks for saving my life." She reached up and kissed him. "Every brave deserves a stallion. Take him for a run."

Charlie put one hand on the rope and gripped its neck. He easily sprang on to the animal's back. He didn't need a saddle. He was Cherokee. They were soon far away.

Sommers and Harold watched the scene quietly with their arms around each other. They slowly moved away from each other, in deep thought.

"I am going and prepare some food for you folk." Annie said.

"I'll come with you," Sommers replied. "I know Charlie will be hungry when he gets back, and PM must be hungry too."

They moved into the kitchen in the bungalow. Harold

went into the tepee. This was his first experience living in a tepee. He liked it. He was surprised at the amount of space it provided, and it was comfortable. The ground was covered with blankets, sweet grass, and fur coats so it was easy underfoot and warm. He removed his shoes. It was nice. The sides of the tepee were pegged down so nothing could crawl in from the outside.

He lay flat and closed his eyes. He was soon asleep. He came awake when Sommers playfully opened his eyelids.

"Wake up sleepyhead. Time to eat."

"What time is it?"

"Almost night time."

"How long has Charlie been back? Have I been sleeping so long?"

"Yes. Come on."

She pulled him up. He put on his shoes and followed her into the bungalow.

It was a nutritious meal. Lots of vegetables, nuts and a salad, and apple cider. They ate quietly. When they were finished, Annie started the conversation.

"Charlie," she said, "I am asking you not to go back to the city."

She stopped speaking and held out her hand to Charlie. He avoided her eyes.

"I want you to stay here with me. There is a lot I have to do, and I need you here with me. I need your strength, and I need your love. I can't do it alone."

She was appealing. Charlie took her hand in his.

"I love you Annie. I know you need me. There are lots of snakes you have to be protected from, and I just received the message that I am your protector and I have to be here for you. I will come back to the reservation, to be close to you."

They kissed. Sommers was all smiles suddenly. She hugged Harold.

"Isn't love wonderful, PM?" She exclaimed. "I found you again, and Annie got back Charlie. I won't have to worry about patching him up anymore, and worrying about where he is and how he is." She laughed. "Annie will take good care of him."

CHAPTER 14

Confession

"What happened with Black Bear?" Harold asked Charlie.

"After Standing Deer's mother and father were left on the Trail of Tears, Black Bear took him under his wing. He was not a full-blooded Cherokee, but was a former slave, a runaway from a white owner. He had been rescued by the Cherokee, had been assimilated by them, and had become part of the tribe, taking part in raids and battles, and adopting their way of life."

"Very interesting.' Harold said.

"Charlie told me this part of his life," Sommers said. "That is what interested me in him, apart from him keeping me busy patching him up at the mission.

"PM, you would not know it, but the entire subject of the ethnic cleansing and genocide of the Indigenous people of North America, slavery of blacks, white and indian, and its many perspectives are part of the study I told you about. I am looking at its different aspects, and how different peoples perceive it and reacted to it, and how it has affected them psychologically, and is still affecting them after all these years. And in addition the case for reparations is still pertinent and in need of resolution.

"But this aspect is extremely complicated, as you pointed out, and I agree with you. The intricacies of the slave trade, slave trading, the role of slaves who became freed and then became slave owners, the intermarriage of African slaves with whites, with Indians, and the distribution of slaves and slave holding among white, Black and Indian.

"In addition the difference between moral and civil rights and justice are involved, and need to be discussed."

"I am really interested in your study and what you have been researching and finding out." Harold said to her.

"I'm glad you're interested PM, because I could use your wisdom and help," she answered.

Annie joined in.

"We Indians have been subjected to the same treatment. We too have been slaves, we kept slaves and our peoples have been massacred by the white man, and its repercussions are still being felt. It has dehumanised most of us. We were subjected to genocide, ethnic cleansing, and robbed of our lands by subterfuge, coerced into signing treaties that are either not kept or are conveniently ignored, and even when we seek to obtain what is rightfully ours we are ignored. We have suffered for hundreds of years and there is no justice.

"However, it's late, and after today's excitement we should all sleep. We can continue this subject tomorrow. Charlie can continue telling us about how Black Bear influenced his life and what else took place on the Trail of Tears."

Sommers yawned and stretched. "It's been an eventful day and I'm tired. Come PM, let's go. Give Annie and Charlie some time to themselves."

Charlie and Annie were in deep discussion when they left the bungalow. She and Harold went into the tepee. They were sleeping lightly, naked under the blankets, with their arms around each other, when Charlie and Annie came into the tepee.

Shortly afterward Harold came awake fully.

The lovemaking between Charlie and Annie, muffled though it was, was still loud enough to be noticeable. Annie did not hide her passion or her excitement.

Sommers also came awake. She heard what was going on. She turned to Harold, and reached for him.

"Kiss me PM," she said.

He kissed her deeply.

"PM, I wanted you from the time when I worked for you long ago. Now I have you back in my life, I don't want to lose you."

"I wanted you too Sommers, but you know the type of man I am. I did not want you to think I might be taking advantage of you, or using my position or anything like that. I'm glad it happened the way it has."

"PM," she said when the excitement had subsided, "I want to take care of you. I love you. I have loved you for a long time. I can't let you out of my life again."

"Since I came back to Toronto you've given me a sense of comfort that I needed. I want you to stay with me, be an important part of my life." he answered.

"Alright my PM." She kissed him.

Annie had pancakes and sausages on the table when they entered the dining area. Charlie was sitting at the table. He looked at them, a mischievous smile on his lips. He reached for the pancakes and shovelled four onto Harold's plate. He poured a copious amount of maple syrup on them. He put an egg and three sausages next to them.

"Eat hearty. While I am with you I am going to become your protector. Can't let you go into the outside world and tell people that we Indians don't know how to take care of you and feed you well."

He turned to Annie who was busy at the stove. "Give PM some coffee," he said. "Do you take milk and sugar PM?" He was very animated, like he had new life. He was happy.

Annie seemed just as happy. She seemed contented, as if a load had been lifted from her shoulders. Her laugh was bell-like as she poured coffee in a mug with the word Seneca written across it, and passed it to Harold.

She sat next to Charlie, brushed her hand lightly through his hair and kissed him lovingly on his cheek. He pulled the long black plaits that fell across her shoulders.

They ate leisurely.

"Tell us about Black Bear, Charlie." Sommers said.

CHAPTER 15

Forced Removal

As Standing Deer related it:

"Black Bear became my father when my parents died. The winter was bitter. I remember looking back out of the wagon I was riding in. Black Bear was putting a coat over my father's shoulder as he sat close to my mother beneath the young pine tree. She tried to wave her hand to me. Sut she was too weak to lift it but I knew she wanted to. Tears would not come to my eyes, but they were there. There was a lump in my throat. I knew I would never see them again. The snowflakes started to drift slowly to the ground. Black Bear came running to the wagon. He reached out to me. He said: 'Your father said goodbye. I am to take care of you. I will protect you from here on.'

I became his son. Since that time he never left my side until he died.

The wagon train had stopped at the outskirts of a heavily wooded area just before they reached Oklahoma. The berry trees were in bloom. Standing Deer was picking some of them, and wandered some distance into the woods. Black Bear had warned him not to go too far into the woods.

He suddenly came face to face with a bear. It was a Black bear. It was as startled as he was. It stood erect. It towered above him. He screamed.

"Black Bear came crashing through the brushes toward it, his hunting knife in his grasp. He ran straight toward the bear, tossing Standing Deer aside as he reached it. He ran under its swinging arms and began stabbing it in its chest. He and the bear toppled to the ground. He kept stabbing it until it stopped moving.

"By this time a number of the braves had come and they finished the bear off. When Black Bear staggered to his feet, he went straight to Standing Deer who was in the arms of one of the elder females of the tribe. He hugged him. There were tears running down his cheeks. It was then that they noticed there was blood running down his shoulder. He was bleeding heavily. One of the braves put him to lie down on the ground. His throat had been slashed by one of the bear's claws. They could not stop the bleeding.

"He reached out for Standing Deer. He couldn't talk. He died before he could hug him.

No one forgot that image. It became an indelible part of Cherokee history and folklore.

Black Bear had given his life for Standing Deer. He was born in another country far away. He was Black. He was not Cherokee, although he became one, and he gave his life for his Cherokee 'son'. Parents lay down their lives for their children.

Charlie became sombre.

"Standing Deer was my grandfather. He taught me all of my Cherokee history. I can never forget the Trail of Tears. I can never forget what it means to be Cherokee. That is why I fight when people denigrate Blacks, Indians or the weak. That is why I was always in fights when I was sent away to boarding school. Even though many of the bullies were bigger than me, those memories gave me the strength to fight them. That is why I am never afraid. Black Bear was not afraid to fight with a bear that was so much bigger than he was.

"I fought how I knew to fight. I learned to defend those who meant something to me and in some cases even those who did not.

"Annie and Sommers," he said to them, "I am sorry I have given you so much trouble putting me back together so often."

Annie was in tears. Sommers wiped her nose with a napkin. She tried to stop the sniffles.

"Kunta Kinte." Harold said softly.

Sommers turned to him. "PM, what do you mean by Kunta Kinte?"

"Do you remember the television series Roots?" he asked quietly.

"Yes," she, Annie and Charlie answered simultaneously.

"Do you remember that when Kunta Kinte was purchased by the white plantation owner and the when overseer asked him his name he said 'Kunta Kinte', his

African name? The overseer angrily told him: 'Your name is Toby!' You have to forget your African name. Your name is Toby.' The overseer was beside himself with anger. Even though Kunta Kinte was beaten many times, almost to death, he refused to give up his African name. He was African, and Africa and would remain African, even if he had to die defending his name and heritage.

"That is why Charlie fights... to preserve his Cherokee heritage, and will defend it to the death. The spirit of Kunta Kinte lives in him. He is defending that part of the African in him also. The spirit of Black Bear."

"That's why I need you around me PM." Sommers said softly. "I need that wisdom to advise me. You pick up these things quickly and can understand people easily. That is the same thing that Pa used to tell me. He admired you as a man of wisdom and vision. When you were campaigning, he always advised me to stick close to you and learn from you. My Pa and Ma really loved you PM."

Annie interrupted the conversation.

"Sommers, I'm coming back to the city with you. When you go back down, I am going to drive behind you, Charlie decided to come back to the reservation with me. I will stay in Toronto a couple of days while he gets his things together.

"Sounds good to me." Sommers said.

"We'll leave in about an hour. That way we won't have to drive too fast. I'm not letting Charlie drive, because he likes to speed. I'm not worried about his driving, but I don't want to be stopped by any police on the highway."

It was almost nightfall when they reached Sommers'

apartment. It was a well-furnished two bedroom apartment with a good view. The kitchen was spacious and well-appointed. The living room could be used for entertainment, and the dining room provided easy access to both kitchen and living room. She had chosen it because although it had been built before many of the newer apartment buildings around, older apartment buildings contained larger rooms. She had always liked bigger rooms because she liked to have space in which to relax. She liked to sit on her balcony at night and watch the cars and trucks whizzing by on the Don Valley parkway, and further north those on the 401 highway.

As soon as they reached home she went to the refrigerator, brought out beers for everyone and put them on the small table on her balcony.

They made themselves comfortable.

"PM," Sommers began the conversation. "All this time from when we arrived at the reservation, you have not taken your eyes off Annie. It's as if you want to ask her something, but you're afraid to ask. Come on, open up and relax, you are among friends. No need for you to be so formal around us."

"I know," Harold answered. "I have no difficulty relaxing with you all. First of all, I am struck by Annie's beauty. Charlie is a lucky man. Then I was wondering how you met. We are so diverse, yet we seem cohesive, as if we are all fighting for the same cause."

Annie drew closer to Charlie.

"It seems that destiny brought us together," she said. "When I read and learned about the massacre of the Sioux at Wounded Knee in 1890, it filled me with indescribable anger. When I read of what took place, I cried. Not once, but every time I read about it."

She paused, took a sip of her beer and continued.

"As a result it motivated me to become a lawyer. I wanted to be able to defend people like Charlie, because I knew what it did to my feelings, and I could understand how it would affect others. When I was in high school I no longer had to attend boarding school like my parents, who were forcibly separated from the rest of the tribe. I became conscious—Indian conscious.

"I was very studious. Every day I thought about our heritage and what had been done to us. I became more focused. I applied for and won scholarships that took me to university, finishing near the top of my class in law school. When I left there I joined a law firm that made it a practice of defending persons who needed help, although all were not necessarily poor. They just needed someone to defend them, since often they could not articulate what was necessary to prove their innocence. That is how I met Charlie and Sommers."

She paused and reached across to kiss Charlie.

"I was in court defending a member of the Seneca tribe—I am a Seneca—who had been brought into court charged with driving under the influence of alcohol. He protested that he was innocent, had protested when he was charged, but the police officers had beaten him and brought him into court, and also charged him with assault and battery of someone who in any case had not turned up to court for the case.

136

"Sommers was the welfare officer assigned to his case. I was able to show that my client was not under the influence of alcohol, but instead was a diabetic, and he was driving erratically because he had not taken his medication earlier in the day, and had not eaten and his glucose level was too low. His case was dismissed.

"I was about to leave court when I noticed this person who I recognized as an Indian, and Sommers. The Indian looked like someone who was about to give up. He seemed resigned to accept whatever punishment was meted out to him. Sommers was talking to him agitatedly and earnestly. He kept shaking his head. There was defiance in its movement. He wasn't saying much. She seemed to be pleading with him. I went over. Here was someone who looked as if they needed help. I had to get involved. I went over to them.

"Can I be of assistance?" Annie asked.

"I am Sommers Blades, social worker assigned to this stubborn man who seems like he wants to go to jail." Sommers replied. "He was involved in a fight. He beat the fellow badly, and was charged with assault and battery. The fellow has not turned up to court. I am telling him to plead not guilty and seek dismissal of the case but he would not listen to me. He is saying that if he has to go to jail he is willing. He says he can't afford any lawyer and whatever sentence he gets he will accept. I keep telling him that is foolishness. But he doesn't want to listen to me."

"My name is Annie Dream-Catcher. I am willing to plead his case. I am willing to appear as amicus curiae, on his behalf. He won't have to pay me."

They spent a few minutes in frantic discussion as she explained the particulars of the charge to Annie.

The Clerk of the Court called out his case. He got up and walked to the dock, his eyes fixed on the floor.

"Charlie Deerfoot," the clerk said, "you have been charged with assault and battery. How do you plead?"

Charlie was about to reply when Annie spoke.

"Your Honour, I am Annie Dream-Catcher of the firm of Broadfoote and Broadfoote, and I appear on behalf of Mr. Charlie Deerfoot. My client pleads 'Not Guilty' to each charge. I would like to point out to the court that the person against whom this assault and battery is supposed to have been committed is not in court, and is thus unable to give evidence. I seek the court's leniency and my client would be grateful if the court would see fit to dismiss the charge, and discharge him."

"I accept your submission," the judge said, "however, I will give a stern warning to him, and also give a word of advice."

The judge turned to Charlie.

"Mr. Deerfoot," he said, "I have read the particulars of the case and the medical reports. It seems that the man was severely beaten, even though you were both fighting. It seems from the police report that you were particularly violent. Had he turned up to give evidence, you faced the possibility of a lengthy term in prison. Thank your legal representative for advocating on your behalf. I am dismissing the charges. My advice to you, though, is for you to try to control your temper in the future. I would recommend you work with your social worker and seek help in anger management and seek counselling. Your case is dismissed."

"Thank you your honour," Annie retorted.

Sommers and Annie got Charlie out of the courthouse as quickly as possible. Annie invited them back to her office where they finished their introductions and got to know each other.

"I was very drawn to him. There was a kindly quality behind that tough exterior."

She looked at him and smiled.

"After that we became friends. I fell in love with him. Every time he got involved in fights I used to patch him up as best I could, until it got too painful for me. I turned him over to Sommers, and went back to the reservation. I couldn't bear the thought of being called sometime to find him in the morgue."

"PM," she suddenly asked Harold, "what do you know of Wounded Knee?"

"Nothing," Harold said, "to be truthful, the only thing I know about Indians is what I used to see in the movie houses back home. I am accustomed to Roy Rogers on the white horse Trigger, Johnny MacBrown who always seemed to be able to shoot seven Indians with his six shooter, and those cowboys who always won whatever the odds. The only movie I saw in which the Indians won was They Died With Their Boots On where Custer and his troops were treated as heroes 'dying with their boots on', although the Indians won. I'm learning, but I need to learn more."

Annie shifted in her seat. She turned to Sommers.

"Sommers, I hope you have lots of beer in the fridge and something to eat. It looks as if tonight will be a long one. It seems he doesn't know anything of the history of the American Indians. We have to teach him."

She motioned to Harold with her glass while saying this. She refilled it and put the empty bottle beside her on the floor. She took a sip from her glass.

"You can't be too hard on him," Sommers replied. "We don't learn much about American history in our English oriented schools, and information about the Indians is scant. I agree with you that he needs educating. Talk to him. I'll prepare some sandwiches."

She turned to Charlie who was trying to watch a baseball game looking sideways through the balcony door leading into the living room.

"What about you Charlie, you alright?"

Charlie didn't reply, he simply held out his empty glass. She filled it, collected the empty bottles, and went into the kitchen.

Annie made herself more comfortable. She continued her narrative.

"PM, you need to learn the truth of how Hollywood continues to distort history and to spread false stories of the Indians. That whole story of the battle at the Little Big Horn is just one of those where the glory belonged to the Indians. They were the heroes. They employed strategies, cunning, and courage, but you will never hear that and no credit will be given to them. Those people will never tell you the whole sordid truth about this civilization that we live in. They will not tell you of the suffering they have caused in this world. They still continue to see us as 'savages'.

"Christians will never tell you of their unchristian treatment of Native people. Historians will never tell you the true history of the white man's massacres, their torture, their dehumanizing actions against disadvantaged people, their genocides. They will seldom tell you of the 'Doctrine of Manifest Destiny', its religious beliefs that propounded the concept that 'God determined that this 'new land' the immigrants from Europe were approaching was to be theirs and theirs alone, to the exclusion of all others, even those who were then living there and had been for hundreds, and even a thousand years before'. As soon as they landed they put this doctrine into practice."

Annie's voice had been increasing in volume and intensity. She stopped.

"I'm sorry PM. I'm truly sorry. I get carried away when I start discussing these things. I am Seneca and my people are among those who suffered and are still suffering. PM, I have lain in my bed and sometimes, in the early morning, before anybody is moving around, when it is still and only the breeze is making a sound, I think about the events at Wounded Knee. I think about those events and wonder about the psychological effects they would have had on the persons involved. I wonder about the state of mind that would have motivated those soldiers to unleash the type of terror they did on those Indians."

She paused. "Do you understand what I am trying to say?"

Harold had been listening with amazement at what he was being told. He was learning. Sommers came back with sandwiches and more drinks. She sat next to Harold on the love seat and reached for his hand.

Annie pulled at Charlie, making him leave the baseball game which had just finished. He pulled his chair back into the group and reached for a drink. Annie continued.

CHAPTER 16

Wounded Knee

The Sioux were being displaced from their lands for a long time on a continuous basis. The government continued to support white settlers who continued to encroach on Indian lands, and the U.S. government facilitated this process by seizing Lakota lands. Attempts by the Indians to protest against this behaviour extended even to the religious rituals that they felt would restore the type of society that conformed to their ideals. Even this was a source of conflict with the white man.

Just as Christians felt that the return of their Messiah would lead to a spiritual awakening, the Sioux spiritual leader Wavoka, started a religious movement based on the 'Ghost Dance', in which they believed that in performing this ritual their 'Messiah' would return, and if they lived righteous lives, life would be as they expected. The bison would return, and the living and the dead would be reunited.

The US Army was adamant that this would lead to Indian uprising and was intent on preventing its performance.

Before the massacre, members of the 7th Calvary came across a number of members of the Lakota at Porcupine Butte and escorted them five miles westward to a camp in Wounded Knee Creek. The remainder of the 7th Cavalry arrived and surrounded the encampment. They were supported by a battery of four Hotchkiss mountain guns (machine guns) which they placed around the encampment.

On December 29th, in the middle of a bitterly cold winter, the troops of the 7th Cavalry went into the camp of the Indians to disarm them. In the attempt a deaf tribesman named Black Coyote, not understanding the instructions, was reluctant to give up his gun. A shot went off during the scuffle. The Army opened fire indiscriminately from all sides with their machine guns, killing men women and children.

Some of the Sioux fled and ran as far away as two miles from the camp, the cavalry pursuing them and killing even those who were unarmed. By the time it was over 150 men, women and children of the Lakota had been killed and 51 were wounded. Estimates placed the number of dead at 300, mostly old men, women and children, and even one baby who was found nursing at her mother's breast. The mother lay dead, and infants were found wandering in the freezing weather, their parents lying dead at their feet.

After the massacre, the bodies were left in the open so that by the time attempts were made to bury them they had been frozen into grotesque shapes and positions. They were buried in a mass grave, still frozen in those shapes.

Grief and disappointment would have resulted in the emotional trauma that existed from then until today. This and other atrocities were perpetrated by the government, including abrogation of treaties signed and promises broken, rations destined for the Indians not given, destitution and starvation the result. Unsanitary and unhealthy food and conditions not fulfilled are some of the factors that provide motivation for the attitudes that led to the standoff that took place as recently as 1973, at the same Wounded Knee.

The battle still continues, because until today the Indian still has a fight to obtain justice. Even today the Seneca, who although not having to endure the psychological trauma of the Sioux because of the massacre at Wounded Knee, have to endure the broken promises and refusal of the government to fulfill the promises that were broken and provide the justice sought.

Even today the Black descendants of Indian African admixture—the Creek Freedmen—cannot get access to what is rightfully theirs in terms of reparations that are paid out to some other Creek descendants, and are denied their justice.

Because Black native Americans did not have written records of their history, they depended on oral history, which naturally changed with the passage of time and retelling. As a result they have been robbed of their history. They don't know who they are or what their ancestors were. The white man is particularly fond of always depicting Blacks as slaves. When Black slaves of the Cherokee were emancipated and freed they were known as the Freedmen and were granted full tribal citizenship. They identified with tribal cultures, spoke tribal languages, intermarried and took part in the religious rites of the Cree.

A Massachusetts Senator, Henry Dawes, who wanted to 'civilize' the Indian territory by ending communal land ownership and allotting 160 acres plots to individual members of each tribe even though the tribes resisted the white man's efforts to destroy the centuries old way of life, applied pressure which resulted in their eventual capitulation "to avoid conflict with the US government. The Dawes Commission resulted in the creation of the 'blood roll', where the census clerks, with no ability to speak the native languages and no ability to differentiate the 'percent of Native blood', resolved the problem through the decision by racially motivated clerks to sometimes divide brothers and sisters into different categories on the roll. They designated members of the same family into Negro and Indian—crude guesswork.

To this day, descendants of the Creek Freedmen complain that "they do not exist in their history". As they say, everyone should have the right to reclaim their heritage.

CHAPTER 17

Dream Catcher

Annie stopped speaking. Charlie reached over the table and kissed her. He turned to Harold.

"PM, do you see why I had to go back to the reservation? This lady is one fantastic person. I have had the chance, since I went back into her hands, to recover myself and regain my equilibrium. I have gone back to work, resuming my profession. I'll bet you didn't know that I am an engineer. I was once employed in a construction company run by the Seneca, but the psychological toll from what we have suffered was too much for me. I took my anger and frustration out through my negative interaction with society. That's why I was always in fights. I became an alcoholic.

"Annie and Sommers saved me. I am more stable now and have learned how to handle my problems. Annie taught me to talk things over with her, and her love keeps me on an even keel."

"Annie," Harold said quietly, "like Charlie I want to learn more from you and Sommers. It seems like each of us needs to regain the paradise we seem to have lost temporarily, for I believe we can. I lost my paradise in that little country in the Caribbean where I was Prime Minister, husband and guide. You and Charlie, your Indian ways of life and the assault on your heritage and culture, and Sommers, her past with loving parents."

"PM," Sommers said, "we will regain our paradise. I am sure of this. We have to be strong enough to fight the obstacles confronting us. You have a role to play in this because you have to help me with my dissertation, and my study of slavery. That way we can each teach those who do not know enough about slavery and its differences."

"Annie," Harold blurted out in the silence that intruded their thoughts. "You have a very interesting name... Dream Catcher... is there a special meaning to it? What little I know about native Indians, I understand that there is usually a meaning to the names your children are given. Why are you named Annie Dream Catcher? What is a Dream Catcher?"

"I wasn't always named Annie."

"What was it? Why did you change it?

"My early name was Sarah. My mother-Flower Moon-made the decision, when I was almost 15 years old. I came home from school one afternoon. Many of the Seneca lived in Oklahoma. One of the many tribes who were moved or rather forced to move there, forced out by the Indian Removal Act, forced to travel the Trail of Tears. We lived on the land designated for us and like so many other tribes we were absorbed by the machinations of the white man's rulings. All the Indians on the continent,

Comanche, Apache Arapaho, Navaho, north, south, east, and west. The buffalo were eliminated, our religion was destroyed, our faith in ourselves, our existence was removed. The Indians were forced to adopt the ways of the white man. Our children were forced to attend the white man's schools, adopt the white man's way of living, and learn the white man's teachings. We were forced to become 'civilized' and adopt a new way of life that was completely foreign to us. Removed to Boarding Schools."

She paused for breath.

"At school the girls were taught to make clothing out of cloth, how to sew, to follow the white man's way, to all dress alike, and look alike. The boys had their hair cut the way the white man looked, and become regimented. We ceased to be Indians. We had no freedom. We were assimilated into the white man's culture. But we were not white. The intention was to destroy us completely. I returned from school, a primary school because I was not yet old enough to attend boarding school. My clothes and belongings were near the door to our cabin.

'We are leaving this place,' Flower moon said quietly.

Where are we going?' I asked.

"We are leaving Oklahoma."

"Why are we leaving?"

"Because you are losing your essence, and I cannot allow that."

"What do you mean?"

"You are Indian." She said looking me steadfastly in my eyes. "Unless you know yourself, you will lose the essence of your being. You will not know who you are. Grandmother has agreed that we should come back to New York, to the Seneca reservation. There you will learn to be an Indian again. She will teach you the way of the Seneca. You will learn who you are, the proud history of the Indian. You will learn who we are. You will be born again."

"My mother," I said with relief because I had been wondering myself for a long time who I was. "I have never been comfortable at the idea of going to the boarding school like you did. I could see that you were not happy."

"Yes my child, I have been unhappy, and I made the decision that you could not be brought up in the same conditions. We will leave tomorrow."

I fell to my knees.

"Thank you my mother." I said. Tears fell from my eyes. I felt like a load had been lifted from my shoulders.

She lifted me to my feet. She wiped the tears from my cheeks.

"When we reach the Seneca reservation, your name will be changed. Grandmother will perform the naming ceremony at the welcoming pow-wow. Your name will be Annie Dream Catcher. Your lessons in being an Indian will begin with that ceremony."

"My mother," I asked, "what is a Dream Catcher?"

"A Dream Catcher is a good luck charm, it is made of feathers beads, willow twigs and is bound together in a special pattern by the chord that holds everything together. When you sleep, the pattern of the knitting lets bad dreams become trapped in the threads, but good dreams pass through the hole in the centre of the pattern. This is the first lesson in your rebirth as an Indian, a true Seneca."

"I will like that name." I said

"You were my good dream," she replied as she gazed over the expanse of Oklahoma territory.

I slept peacefully that night.

PART 3

CHAPTER 18

Mamuza

Mamuza's memory of life before her enslavement, before she was taken from her African village until the Indian came into her life, was a series of fleeting memories behind a hazy, diaphanous black curtain. It presented in her brain as a picture of a forest and rolling brown earthen hills, heavy rains and fields of corn and vegetables that she and other members of her village planted and reaped and ate—that sustained them.

Then the men came. Strong black men with spears and clubs, speaking a different tongue. The men captured them, bound them to each other by their necks and marched them out of the village. This was the village of dead and dying men who could not help them; men who fought valiantly but were overwhelmed.

They were marched many days through the forest.

When they reached the castle they were taken into the dungeons beneath it. The dungeon was dank and damp. Its thick walls were covered with dirt and excrement. It was sickening. The iron door kept even fresh air away from them.

The curtain shifted and the deafening sound of the surf, each wave mounted by the long boats propelled by the muscular shoulders of the black bodies pulling the long oars, soon gave way to the calmer, deeper water where the bigger ship with the big white sails towered above them.

Strong arms that had seized them when they were led out of the dungeon, squinting in the strong sunlight as they came out, now placed them in the long boats, now seized them and hoisted each of them out of their boat on to the deck of this monster. The brief respite from the bonds was soon replaced by the chains which once more bound them to each other. Darkness overwhelmed her as she was pushed into the bowels of the monster and made to lie down in the cramped space with all the other blacks in this blackness.

The blackness, the stench, the cries, the sobbing, the moaning, the babble of various languages were her constant companions, growing louder and rising in intensity when the rolling of the monster brought them to the realization that it was moving.

There was no going back. The coast of Africa was giving way to a memory, growing distant with the passage of time.

Days passed. People died from sickness. Those too sick to help themselves were thrown overboard to the sharks that were constant companions of the monster. The haze kept other memories hidden, so she didn't know or remember the difference between one day and another, one meal and the other, or when they were fed—not often, what it tasted like or how it entered and exited her body.

As she lay trembling in its bowels, the monster rolled and groaned as if it wanted to expel her, and she retched trying to expel what was not inside of her bowels. There was nothing there. She was sea sick.

Days and nights passed. What little food was given was sickening in looks and worse in taste. At first she didn't want to eat, but as time passed she realized that she had to eat or die from hunger. She wanted to live. She ate.

Days and nights passed. Her sense of smell was heightened as time passed, until a new smell entered her consciousness. It was the smell of land, and also a sweet aroma, one she did not recognize.

The splash of the anchor and the slowing of the monster until it stopped resulted in another activity taking over. The slaves were unchained from each other, although their wrists were still attached to their chains. They blinked their eyes, more accustomed to the gloom of the monster's bowels but now unfocussed in the brilliant sunshine.

Boats were lowered over the side of the ship and the women and children placed in them. In contrast to the black skins that had brought them out to the monster at the beginning of her ordeal, the oars were now manned by ugly, smelly, dirty white men. They soon reached the warehouses on the wharf. They were offloaded and the boats returned for another load of slaves. The enslaved huddled together in a corner of the large shed where they had been taken.

The air was sweet. She didn't know it at the time, but

this place changed the long stalks of the sugar cane plant into crystals of sugar, and the air was permeated with the sweet aroma as the juice was boiled to produce the crystals.

Mamuza was pushed roughly through the gate at the entrance to a narrow lane between the two buildings, out through the gate at the end and into the space in the other building. Slaves were made to stand on a platform and were brought forward to a smaller platform from time to time. White men examined each one that was brought forward. Some white women were there also.

The white people spoke a language she did not understand.

Mamuza's turn came. The white men seemed more excited when she stood on the platform. They gesticulated more and shouted louder. When it ended she was led away by a white man and a black one who was much younger.

Then she was put on the mule-drawn wagon. The young black man drove the wagon while the white man sat next to him on the wooden plank that served as a seat for them. It was carrying a load of grass, and travelled along a rough gravel road. Though the road was rough, the rocking seemed like the swaying of the boat she had travelled on, and she fell asleep. It was more comfortable than the place she had been before, and the grass smelled sweet. She didn't know how long she had been sleeping, but she awoke when it stopped.

The white man jumped off. He was stocky and

paunchy. He wore a white suit, carried a straw hat, and had a cigar perched on one side of his mouth. His thin downturned lips made him appear to be constantly angry, and his deepest eyes beneath overhanging, bushy blonde, eyebrows were difficult to fathom.

He stood to one side of the cart when the young black man helped her down. She stood next to it in bewilderment. She looked around. Smoke was coming from a chimney in the yard, and the sweet smell she had earlier encountered when the monster stopped was also coming from the large shed where a number of people like her were bringing the bundles of the long grass stalks that they pushed under the crushers turned by the huge sails of the windmill. As she turned and looked around, she realized the place was on a hill. On one side she could see waves from the ocean coming into shore. A touch of nostalgia came across her consciousness, as she realized that these were like the waves that had pounded against the shore when she had been first captured and taken to the monster. It was like home in Africa.

The white man shouted. She couldn't understand his language. A large black woman appeared from a house behind the windmill and came to him. She bowed her head as he began to speak. She lifted it after a while and came over to Mamuza. She put her arms around her and led her away. The younger man and the mule cart had disappeared. The white man went into the room from which the smell came. The older woman led her into the back of the house.

It was a large house with a verandah spreading across

its length, facing the incoming waves and the breeze blowing off the ocean.

Mamuza didn't have time to fully observe the house. She was taken to the back of the building to a smaller cabin, a single room with grass spread in one corner. The woman took her there and motioned her to lie on it. She sank on it, grateful for the chance to rest. She fell asleep again.

It was almost nightfall when she awoke. As she opened her eyes she saw the older woman sitting on a rickety chair at a small table, looking at her. Wordlessly the woman came over, lifted her, brought her to another equally rickety chair at the table and handed her a bowl with a stew and mashed green banana.

Mamuza was very hungry. She started to eat, but before she could eat very much, the older woman stopped her. She indicated that Mamuza should take her time and not eat too much right away.

"I am Tituba," the older woman said to her. "I am Ibo."

Surprise registered on Mamuza's face. She was also Ibo. Here was a chance to speak her own language. As she ate she thought of her good fortune. All things considered, she had been taken captive and had endured the long sea voyage, but she was alive and now was with someone with whom she could converse. As the hot food settled in her stomach, she began to feel better and relaxed more.

She finished eating, placed her head on her arms at the table, and was soon asleep.

It was raining heavily when she awoke. There was a single room divided by a string running from one side to the other, dividing it into sleeping and eating sections.

Tituba brought a bucket of rain water that she dipped from a large barrel outside the entrance to the cabin, and handed it to her.

"Wash," she simply said.

"Alright auntie." Mamuza felt good hearing her language and her heart warmed to the mellifluous voice. She was hearing it for the first time in a long time.

She was handed some clothes, and when Mamuza removed what she was wearing, Tituba gathered them up and placed them in a bundle by the entrance to be discarded.

She talked to Mamuza while she was washing herself.

"You have been brought to this place. It is an island called Barbados, and you are owned by the white man who brought you home. His name is Massa Drayton. Everyone and everything around here is owned by Massa Drayton. The driver of the mule cart is Ishi. You will meet him. He speaks our language, and he will teach you to talk like Massa Drayton, to speak his language. He is to take us to see Massa Drayton at the plantation house.

Tituba gave her a tin cup with a sweet smelling tea made from an aromatic plant growing by the entrance. Ishi came to the door and she gave him a cup also. He drank his, standing at the entrance. His gaze was fixed on Mamuza. He nodded to her. She nodded back.

The rain had stopped. They climbed on the mule cart and were soon at the kitchen entrance to the house. Drayton was sitting in an armchair in the large dining room located just off the kitchen when they entered.

"Morning Massa," Tituba said to him.

He said nothing in return. He just looked at Mamuza. He signaled for her to stand in front of him, and then for her to spin round. She kept her eyes lowered, and stood with her hands in front with her fingers intertwined. He used his brass handled walking stick to lift her skirt. She first thought of resisting him, but she remembered Tituba's words and that she was the property of the man before her. She let him have his way. He smiled when there was no resistance. He owned her.

He said something to Tituba, who gave a lengthy response. He said something else, and waved his hand in dismissal.

"Come Mamuza," Tituba said, "Massa say he glad he buy you. You is to work in de kitchen with me, you is to help cook, work in de yard, and in de boiler house and in de crusher, where you see people loading the canes. You is to live in de cabin wid me, but we got to get Massa breakfast first, so help me light dis stove and get the food.

She showed Mamuza where to get things, how to light the big cast-iron stove, where to get the food, and she began her new education.

When everything including Drayton's breakfast was finished, and the dishes gathered up, she led Mamuza outside the kitchen and down the steps of the large building. There were a large number of people working in the yard. Mule carts loaded with cane were unloading the long stalks at the entrance to the crushers, pushing them under the huge wheels turning by the sails of the large windmill driven by the constant breeze coming off the ocean. They never stopped.

Ishi was tending the mules of one of the carts when they passed. He looked up and smiled. Mamuza quickly looked away. However, she began to feel comfortable for the first time since she had been captured. Her life now seemed more determined. She decided to offer libations to her private Orishas, especially those who had protected her so far.

"All of this," Tituba said motioning all around her, "all of these people, an land an property, belong to Massa Drayton. And that ent all, he got property overseas, that he does go an visit sometimes. Massa Drayton very rich."

CHAPTER 19

Carolina

Life took on a distinct pattern after that. Her daily duties were not unduly strenuous or difficult. Tituba was kind and understanding. It was only when Drayton decided to entertain some of his friends and acquaintances among the other plantation owners that it became very hectic.

The plantation owners Drayton entertained were a select group. These were part of the group who had left the island a number of years earlier and gone to settle a part of the North American continent, a group who had settled in the 'Low Country' of the American mainland south of Georgia which they named 'Carolina' after the ship that took them there. The expedition was led by John Yeaman, a colourful and resourceful leader who was not only an explorer and adventurer, but once fought a duel over a married woman lover. Yeaman not only killed the husband, but later married the dead man's wife and returned to Barbados.

The colony did well at the beginning exporting boards, shingles and other products back to Barbados. Relations with the Indians—the Machapungo, Croatan/

Hatteras, who in the early 1700s merged to become the Mettamuskeets—was harmonious at the beginning. Sexual unions between the Yeaman colonists and the descendants of the Croatans resulted in offspring not only in the Albermerle region, but some are still in Barbados today. It is believed that the Mettamuskeet Indians fomented the uprising that led to the rest of the Indians in the Yamasee war in opposition to the Native American Slave trade.

Archeological evidence identifies a close relationship between the inhabitants of Yeaman's colonists and the Indians, and there is evidence that a plague identified as the Black-Tongue Plague that in 1840 wiped out a large number of people from the colony, was most likely Anthrax imported from Barbados. At that time cattle and pigs were traded for naval stores between the two populations. After that the survivors of the colony moved away and never came back.

[[chapter break]]

The moon was full and just rising, like a large golden ball over the eastern horizon. It was peaceful. The foam-capped waves were following each other in single file, ending their march silibantly on the sloping sand of the many bays this side of the island. Mamuza was sitting beneath the Casuarina trees, her favourite place, watching the scene before her. Tituba came out of the cabin.

"Mamuza," Tituba said to her, "why are you here alone?"

"I am looking at my homeland," she answered.

"And what are you seeing?"

"I am seeing my life as a free young woman. I am trying to learn what it is to be a slave."

Mamuza turned to the older woman.

"Auntie," she said using the greeting of respect usually used by Africans when addressing older persons. "Can you tell me, Auntie, how one endures being a slave? Can you teach me how to swallow myself so that I do not destroy myself by not wanting to be a slave, but having to be a slave? Massa Drayton call me to his room some nights ago and lay on top of me. It hurt. He was cruel. I wanted to go and throw myself over the cliff, but I could not. I want to live, but why do I find it difficult to do so?"

Tears ran down her cheeks. She continued.

Then I saw him beat Longo today. I wanted to rebel against his cruelty, but I realized I am a slave and could do nothing. My Orisha held me back. It would not let me rush at Massa Drayton."

Tituba looked at the pretty young woman sitting beside her, her beauty becoming more revealing every day. She was maturing as she grew stronger, but the sadness never left her eyes. She was learning quickly.

As Ishi taught her, she was beginning to understand Massa Drayton's language more and more, and now she was beginning to read and write as Ishi taught her, either in the cabin by candle light, or in the quiet evenings when the mill was not grinding any cane.

Ishi was patient. He was falling in love.

Tituba was silent. The question she was being asked required an answer, but she didn't know how to answer it.

Mamuza continued. "I lay on my bed at night, and as the wind blows through the shak-shak trees they talk to me, and soothe me. After I make obeisance to my Orishas they talk to me also, and I become calm, and I sleep."

Tituba looked up at the needle-like leaves of the casuarinas above them. She sighed.

"Mamuza, I do not know how to answer your question. I was born a slave. My father and my mother were both owned by Massa Drayton father. I was born on this plantation, and since they were owned by Mass Drayton father, he get to own me too. I become his property.

I cannot even swim in the bay, because I cannot swim so there is no place for me to swim to. I gots to stay here till I die. I don't even know what it is like to be free. Tell me what it is like to be free Mamuza. I cannot even go to another plantation, because if a slave is found off the plantation lands, the Massa can take whatever revenge he want, and there is nothing the slave can do. I don't even want to have no children for Massa Drayton to get to own. So I learn how to use 'lignum vitae', an every time I going to get a child for he, I learn what to do. The women in the boiling house talk to me an tell me what to do. I can't stop he from lying pun top of me. All like now I don't feel nothing. I know what he going want to do wid you. That is why he buy you. But I going show you what to do. I going take care of you."

"That would be nice, Auntie, cause he does try to 'do' with me often in the house. I feel helpless. I have no one to love me."

Tituba reached out and hugged her. "I love you chile."

Silence, like a warm blanket, reached out to the two women and they took comfort in each other's thoughts. They were the same, wrapped in the arms of loneliness. They longed to be free—Mamuza because she had once been free, and Tituba because she had never been free, and had never known freedom. She was born a slave, and that is all she knew about.

Mamuza's education progressed quickly under Tituba's guidance.

Drayton was a hard taskmaster with the slaves working on the plantation and producing the sugar. It had been a good year and the crop season after Mamuza's arrival had been a good profitable one.

Mamuza and Ishi got closer to each other and fell in love. He was warm and tender when they were together—not like Drayton—and when they swam naked in the warm water of the bay beneath the plantation house and made love by the light of the moon, she forgot that she was confined to the plantation.

Visits by other plantation owners, especially those who like Drayton had property in Carolina, became more frequent. Tituba alerted Mamuza about her suspicions of what was taking place.

"Mamuza," she said one afternoon, "I think Massa preparing to go to his plantation in Carolina, so don't be surprised if he suddenly say he leaving. Prepare yourself.

I know he going take you with him."

She prepared herself, but it was still a surprise when he suddenly announced one morning that they were going to Drayton Hall.

They put her in the row-boat and carried her along the short drive out to another 'monster'. They hoisted her onto its deck and with a loud snap the sails of the monster filled with air and it began to move over the waves.

The land, when she looked back, was fading into the distance as the sea became darker and the rolling waves passing underneath became bigger. She was once more forced into the bowels of the monster. There were fewer people this time.

As she lay trembling in its bowels it rolled and groaned as if it wanted to expel her, and she retched trying to expel what was not inside of her own bowels. There was nothing there. She was sea sick again.

Darkness fell. Through the grating above her head she could see the stars. At one point she could see the Southern Cross. Her grandfather in Africa had taught her to follow the stars to find her way back home. She could still remember, and she knew the monster was going north, further away from the place of the sweet smell where she had once stood on the auction platform.

Loneliness overwhelmed her. There was no Tituba around to comfort her. She pulled Anoush closer to her side. She believed that if she didn't have the child she would probably have thrown herself into the raging sea beneath the storm-tossed ship.

Parting from Tituba was painful, but Anoush needed her.

Massa Drayton's announcement that he was going to Carolina was sudden and heart wrenching. She knew nothing about the new country, and Tituba was of no help. She had never left Barbados, so she couldn't give any advice apart from the comfort of her arms while they could be with each other.

Ishi was nowhere around. Massa Drayton had sold him to the Middleton plantation a few years before when she had given birth to the child. Throughout her pregnancy he had treated her kindly in the belief she was carrying his child.

When the baby was born—delivered by Tituba in the cabin—and he realized it was a black girl child and enquiries revealed that Ishi was the father, he became incensed. He whipped Ishi in the plantation yard in front of all the workers, in front of the boiling house where the sugar cane was changed through boiling from the juice of the crushed stalks to the sweet crystals of sugar. They had to be boiled to change.

She felt every lash, but she was proud of him. He never uttered a sound. He just kept looking at her until he lost consciousness. She was glad it was his child. Ishi was strong, brave and yet kindly.

She never knew when he was taken away from the plantation. He was gone. He never told her how he found out she was going to Carolina. She just knew he was beside her the night before she left.

Maybe it was the drums.

On their last night together they were both tearful. He was tender and they were together as a family for that time only. Then he was gone in the darkness just before dawn.

Tituba provided comfort and advice until she too was gone. Reverend Parris, the bible-thumping firebrand preaching the need for redemption, bought her after spending an evening at the plantation. He convinced Drayton that he needed her to provide for him when he was going to Massachusetts. He took her away late one evening.

Mamuza was grief-stricken. Then she received the news that they were going to Carolina. She, Anoush and some other house workers would be needed to cater to Drayton.

Days and nights passed. Her sense of smell was heightened as time passed until the new smell entered her consciousness. It was the smell of land, not the fresh aroma like the place she had been taken from, or even her homeland, but a new dank odour of swampland. The monster stopped. With a splash of the anchor, a different activity took over.

All the slaves were pulled and pushed on to the deck. Mamuza looked around. All she could see was swampland, although she could see what appeared to be a series of houses in the distance. Boats were lowered over the side and women and children placed in them. In contrast to the black skins that had prodded them into the monster at the beginning of her captivity, the oars were now manned by ugly, dirty, smelly and in some cases toothless, white men.

They were offloaded on to the docks and the oars returned for another load. Now they were on the shore of Carolina.

CHAPTER 20

Drayton Hall

Mamuza and Anoush sat in the bottom of the carriage that left the docks with the slaves, while Drayton sat on the seat above them. The carriage was pulled by a couple of fine black horses whose reins were controlled by a black coachman dressed in satin shirt and who carried a fine whip. The animals held their heads proudly and matched their steps perfectly. They were well trained. They quickly traversed the long, tree-lined driveway.

The coachman stopped the carriage. Drayton stood up and looked all around the surrounding fields of cotton stretching as far as the eye could see. Slaves, male and female and some children, appeared. They were soon joined by a person on horseback, a stout grizzled white man whose face showed the evidence of too much whisky. The overseer, obviously.

"Welcome home Massa Drayton," he bowed.

"I'm glad to be back Stanley."

"You will see that everything is in order when I give you an accounting."

"The woman here is Mamuza," Drayton said to him.

"She will look after the house and cooking. We will put things in better order when we are all settled."

Tituba had taught Mamuza well during the time they had been together. Within a short time she turned Drayton Hall into a shining example of efficiency and elegance. Everyone admired it. Drayton was pleased, and showed it, especially when he entertained. People deliberately made it an occasion to visit, or pass by the house, showering Drayton with their compliments.

Anoush was growing into a lovely young woman and Mamuza kept a steady eye on her and kept her as close as possible, especially when an increasing number of men began to visit.

And then she was gone. Mamuza returned from the peach orchard and could not find her. She frantically searched, she asked questions, but could get no answers. She questioned Drayton, but he seemed disinterested.

She thought this was strange because based on what Tituba had told her about slavery, Anoush was his property and the loss didn't seem to be too important to him.

For weeks Anoush couldn't be traced. Mamuza could not regain her equilibrium. She had no desire to do any work. Anoush was part of her soul.

Months passed. And then she heard the drums. There was a constancy in their beating during the stillness of the night. There seemed to be an urgency about them, the beating was different. It was a different message. She visited the slave huts and asked questions about the drumming. She had forgotten the codes and needed to be reminded of them.

The messages came through. Anoush was alive.

She was living with the Cherokee Indian, one who had visited Drayton many times, and was now part of the Cherokee tribe far away. Drayton had sold her to the Indian. Mamuza would never see her again.

She remembered the Indian. He was tall and well muscled. He seldom spoke although Drayton was always talking to him. He had been a frequent visitor to Drayton Hall, and she remembered the way he looked at Anoush. Recently his visits had become more frequent and he spent many days and evenings there. Whenever he came he seldom kept his eyes away from Anoush very long. Mamuza tried to keep her away from his presence as often as she could by finding work for her to do either in the adjoining laundry house, or in the kitchen. But Drayton always tried to find work for her to do in their presence.

Mamuza became fearful, and now the drums told her that her fears had been well founded. She had one consolation—she had taught Anoush how to look after herself. She had taught her to be strong mentally and physically. She had taught her how to make libations to the ancestors to give her guidance and to make obeisance to the Orishas to give her comfort and courage. Anoush was in good hands. Her Orishas would look after her.

Drayton had sold Anoush to the Indian. This shocked her.

She became more deliberate in her preparations. She became more silent and withdrawn, but she spent many months in her planning. She had decided on her path.

Then she was ready.

That evening she took special care. She bathed leisurely. She was well oiled and perfumed when she went into the room.

He was aware of a presence. A slight movement at the door of the dining room attracted his attention. He smelled her. Mamuza was framed by the doorway. Her well-oiled skin shone in its nakedness, reflected in the mirror in its opulent frame by the large candelabra and the kerosene lamps of the room. It was early evening, a soft summer evening. The tree frogs and crickets were playing their music.

"Massa want Mamuza?" Her voice was soft and seductive.

"Massa want Mamuza?" She repeated the invitation. He shifted in his seat at the table to bring her into better focus. He became aroused as he saw her fully. She always had that effect on him. From the time he saw her on the auction block, he had to have her. He knew he was right from the time he first lay with her.

She was unwilling and cried, but he ignored her. She was his property and there was nothing she could do about it. He had his way with her. Afterward she gave in, and although he knew she was unwilling to show him any affection, he didn't mind that. He got his own satisfaction just by having her. Now she was offering herself to him. He became more aroused. He began to rise slowly, but she held out her hand and stopped him.

"Massa," she said a bit louder. "Massa, you want

Mamuza?"

She didn't wait for his answer, she turned and locked the door behind her. Drayton stopped. There was something different in her demeanour. He noticed the whip in her hands.

"MASSA DRAYTON," the intensity of her voice had increased. "Massa Drayton," she asked, "WHERE ANOUSH? WHERE MAMUZA CHILD?"

Drayton became angry. Who was this woman to be questioning him? He owned her. How dare she question him?

"I sold her to the Indian! He needed someone to be companion to his wife, so I sold her to the Indian."

"MASSA---SELL---ANOUSH---TO THE INDIAN!?" Her voice rose. The drums had not lied. She knew they were right for certain now.

"MASSA SELL MAMUZA CHILD, FLESH OF MAMUZA FLESH, TO THE INDIAN? Mamuza carry Anoush for months as part of Mamuza. Anoush is part of Ishi. She belong to us, and you sell her to the Indian? MASSA DRAYTON, YOU GOTS TO PAY FOR THAT."

She tossed the key to the room aside.

She flicked her wrist and the whip snaked out. He felt a sting on one of his cheeks. He put his hand there and recoiled when he realized there was blood on it. The whip snaked out again and he felt it wrap around his shoulder. The pain shocked him. When her wrist moved again he felt it on his back. Mamuza had practised well with the whip, and she was strong and expert in its use.

Blood came from the other cheek.

He tried to grab it when it moved again and curled around his neck. He tried to pull it out of her hands, but when he did he found that she had braided pieces of glass within the strands of rawhide. He also realized her strength. His hands were bleeding. He couldn't hold it, he had to let it go. He tried to escape its wrath, but it would not be denied, it followed him around the room. There was no escape. She took her fury, her frustrations, her hatred, her hurt out on him.

"THESE ARE FOR LONGO!"

The whip cracked three more times, creating more gashes across his back. His shirt was in tatters. He cringed behind one of the high chairs. She dragged it away from him and the tray with wine glasses and red wine fell to the floor, mixing with the bloody drops from his body. The whip found him three more times and blood flowed even more. Its snap and crackle were loud in the stillness of the silent mansion.

"THESE ARE FOR ISHI, THE FATHER OF MY CHILD! Now you will know how Ishi felt when you beat him."

More lashes followed. Drayton knew that he could not live. She intended to kill him. There was no one to come to his assistance. Drayton Hall stood by itself, isolated in its opulence and size.

He cowered out of fear and whimpered because of the pain. Her gleaming white teeth, bared and snarling, were bright in the darkness and shadows of the room.

"MASSA SELL ANOUSH TO THE INDIAN? WHAT GIVE YOU THE RIGHT TO OWN MAMUZA? WHAT GIVE YOU

THE RIGHT TO OWN MAMUZA CHILD? MAMUZA HAD A MOTHER AND FATHER. MAMUZA HAD A FAMILY AND RELATIVES. MAMUZA WAS FREE TO RUN IN THE FOREST AS SHE WANTED TO. YOU, AND PEOPLE LIKE YOU, MAKE MAMUZA A SLAVE. WHAT GIVE YOU THE RIGHT? BECAUSE MAMUZA BLACK!!!?"

The whip never stopped in its movement coming from all directions: up down and across. Blood came from wherever it touched on his body.

Drayton collapsed.

"DRAYTON!!" she screamed, "MASSA DAY DONE!! MASSA DAY DONE!!"

She flicked her wrist and the lighted candles caught the drapes afire. She threw the lighted kerosene lamp at him. It exploded in flames.

Drayton Hall was burning. Drayton wasn't aware of anything. Mamuza was breathing heavily from her exertion. She was smiling as the burning beam fell on her head. The whip was still in her hand.

"MASSA DAY DONE..." she whispered, "Massa...day...done!"

CHAPTER 21

Ishi

The drums told the story. They were beating furiously throughout the night and early morning. Drayton Hall had burned to the ground. Mamuza and Drayton were both dead. Ishi was deep in the woods of South Carolina, Cherokee territory, when he heard them. He was happy for Mamuza. Now she would be free from the turmoil of her life as a slave. In all the time they had spent together, she had always bemoaned the fact that she was a slave.

Ishi understood, for he also suffered that same torment. He wanted to be free and was always seeking to find ways to obtain this freedom. The scars on his back were a constant reminder of what Drayton had done to him, and this hatred increased whenever he thought of the child he had fathered, the woman he loved, and the inability to be himself. He belonged to someone.

Middleton, his new master after the whipping and his sale to his new master, was better to him than Drayton. Although kindly, he was a hard taskmaster. He had a wife and children, a boy and two daughters. Middleton's plantation was some distance away from Drayton's in Barbados, and after he took Ishi away, having bought him cheaply from Drayton, he had him nursed back to health and gave him light work to do when he was fully recovered. He was only on the plantation in Barbados for a few months afterward. Middleton's plantation in Carolina needed someone of Ishi's strength and size to assist in its smooth functioning. Middleton's decision to visit his plantation overseas was made after news reached him that there was the possibility of a rebellion among the slaves. He was not as wealthy as Drayton and the plantation was a significant investment he could not afford to lose. His plans were made and preparations for his voyage included taking Ishi, now fully recovered from Drayton's whipping and having regained his strength. Ishi provided him with the added support he felt he needed to control his slaves.

After reaching the Carolina plantation without adverse effects after the storm that battered their ship for a couple of days, he put Ishi in charge of producing the indigo for which Middleton's plantation was famous. In addition to indigo large tracts were devoted to sugar cane production and to cotton. Middleton's slaves were relatively content, but there were always rumours of discontent. There was a restlessness among them, a discontent that was spreading among the plantations with African slaves throughout the South, and Indian raids on the plantations meant that everyone had to be constantly on watch.

They came during the early hours of a weekend. The

temperature was hot and sleep kept their eyes closed until the hollering and whooping announced their presence. The Indians came directly to the plantation house and the stables. They set fire to the thatched roof and opened the doors, chasing the horses into the forest. The slaves in general cowered in their huts, not daring to venture out. They soon realized, however, that they were not the object of the raid. The Indians were primarily after the horses and some of the cattle on the plantation.

When the raid began Ishi quickly pulled on his clothes and prepared to jump through one of the windows. As he opened it he came face to face with a fierce-looking warrior with his face smeared with black war-paint holding a tomahawk and about to strike. They looked at each other. It was as if they each looked in a mirror. They were the same.

The Indian quickly turned and ran toward the stables chasing after a horse that was running past. Ishi ran toward the stable where Middleton kept his prized thoroughbreds. He quickly put a rope around the neck of the best of the stallions, jumped on its back, and putting a rope around another, galloped out after the Indians, galloping off into the woods with all the other horses.

Middleton's allies, some other owners who had been visiting, laid down a barrage of gunfire that soon scared them off. The slaves rushed to extinguish the fires that had been set and order was restored. Ishi was missing, however. No one knew what had become of him. He was gone.

Middleton resigned himself to the loss of his trusted

servant. He assumed that Ishi was captured by the Indians or killed somewhere. The horses could and would be replaced.

Life soon returned to normal on the plantation, but everybody missed Ishi. He had become popular among the slaves because he was kind. Despite his size and strength there was a gentleness about him that made them want to keep him happy.

A large profit was made from the indigo, the prices for the reaped sugar cane was good and there were no more raids on the plantation.

Middleton was pleased with the administration and running of the plantation, and he soon made plans to return to Barbados.

Then he heard of the occurrences at Drayton Hall. He was sorry for Drayton, but he was not really very sympathetic. He felt that Drayton was responsible for his own undoing because of his treatment of his slaves. Drayton always maintained that he got more out of his slaves, and this was symbolic of the treatment of the slaves by many of the plantation owners. He was always of the opinion that things would get steadily worse with the passage of time if cruelty was not maintained.

Ishi had no difficulty following the Indians. Dawn was just breaking when the raiders arrived at the village where they had established their camp. There was happiness among the rest of the camp at the result of the raid. They had captured many horses and cattle with few losses of their own.

Ishi had been sitting on his horse while the celebration was taking place. One brave noticed him and raised the alarm. Many of them raised their weapons, but watched him carefully.

They fell silent as he approached leading the horse he had brought with him. He held up his hands to show he carried no weapons, and simply said:

"Chief."

Excitement grew as he drew nearer. A warrior approached to take the horse he held but he pulled the rope away and repeated: "Chief."

A warrior with a headdress of eagle feathers came out of one of the tepees. He approached Ishi as the hollering from the other warriors continued.

Ishi approached him. Without descending from his horse, he held out the rope of the horse he was leading.

"Yours," he said, releasing the rope.

The chief took it, and as it stood quietly he walked all around it. He shouted something Ishi did not understand.

A woman approached, holding a birch bark bowl with a porridge of maize. Ishi dismounted and took it. He drank from the bowl. He became part of the Cherokees who had raided Middleton's plantation. He became Cherokee.

CHAPTER 22

The Indian

Anoush and the Indian travelled in silence along the forest trails, heading in a northerly direction. The pace was unhurried. He looked at her from time to time, but she avoided his eyes. She kept her head bowed. She was sad, but unafraid.

Mamuza had taught her to be steadfast, to analyze situations, and to refrain from using her energies to resist situations she could not control and from which she could not escape.

Her sale to the Indian and her removal from the plantation, from Drayton Hall, was one of those situations. She determined to accept it as it was and act according to what was available to be used to her advantage. As she grew she learned to be resourceful. She had learned to develop her strength so that even though she was relatively young, she could handle herself through her versatility.

They travelled throughout the day. Their only conversation took place after they had travelled for over an hour.

They came to a stream and he stopped the cart. It was on the banks of a quiet stream gurgling over a pebble-filled watercourse. He helped her down from the cart, and while the horses drank from the stream, he unloaded some supplies from the cart. She relieved herself in the bushes behind a large Birch tree.

When she returned he handed her a piece of beef jerky and a water jug with water. She drank thirstily and paused to take a bite of the jerky. They were in a heavily wooded area surrounded by pine and birch trees. The underbrush was not so thick that it presented difficulty for the cart and the horses to make steady progress when the journey began again. They travelled faster now. It was more purposeful and night was descending quickly.

The Indian reached out his hand and helped her board the cart again. He seemed almost gentle when their hands touched. His voice surprised her. It was deep, almost guttural, but there seemed to be a hesitance in his approach to her.

"You not have to be afraid. I will not hurt you. Me Indian. Good man, not like Drayton. Drayton white man. Bad man. Drayton want to hurt you. I buy so that Drayton not able to hurt you."

He looked into the distance ahead as if he was studying the clouds gathering ahead of them. He urged the horse to move faster.

"Have to reach near edge of forest before moon time."

Anoush did not comment, but his concern registered with her. His concern seemed genuine, and deep inside she agreed with him about his comments on Drayton.

186

Over the years as she grew up Drayton's cruelty was seen in his treatment of his unpaid for labour force. Deep down inside, now that she had been in the company of the Indian, she was beginning to feel more comfortable. She was glad to be away from Drayton Hall. She missed Mamuza though.

The sun was beginning to set behind the hills they were approaching. The valleys intertwined with small rivers and streams. They reached a clearing on the banks of another stream.

The Indian halted. He helped her down from the cart and started to set up camp for the night. He took his Tomahawk and began to clear the area, cutting pine boughs to make a bed for her, pulling sweet grass to put over them and covering them all with a deerskin hide. He placed a circle of rocks he took from the stream, and soon had a fire going within that circle. He went a little distance into the woods and soon returned with a rabbit which he skinned and shortly after had it turning on a spit above the fire. Next to the fire he set a small pot of water into which he put some coffee. Within a short time he handed her a tin cup with coffee and a piece of the now cooked rabbit.

She was hungry, and felt even better when the food entered her stomach. She had a feeling of gratitude for this Indian who had shown her a side of these people that she had never been exposed to. Whenever Drayton and other plantations met at Drayton and discussed the Indians, they were always describing them as 'savages', who to them should not even exist in their own country.

Now she was seeing exactly who these people were. Their highly bronzed colour—almost as dark as hers—and gentle manner toward her contrasted with the picture always being painted of these people.

She felt her admiration for this man beginning to grow. When she began to doze off, lying on her bed of pine boughs, her last view of him before her eyes closed was his silhouette against the flames of the fire, looking over the hills they would reach the next day.

He had pointed this out, saying: "Reach home tomorrow, midday. You meet my people. Meet my sister and father and mother. You will like."

"Would be nice, I miss my mother Mamuza," she replied hesitantly.

She looked back along the trail they had traversed. That was the last time she looked back. She never mentioned Mamuza again.

She was surprised when, on her way to the stream to wash before the beginning of the day, she saw him in the shade of a large pine tree. He was surrounded by smoke, and appeared to be washing himself with the smoke emanating from a bowl of burning herbs using an eagle feather to perform this 'sacred' task. Just as she offered libations to the ancestors, and offered obeisance to her Orishas, the Indian was praying to his great father, and giving his own thanks to the superior being. They were the same.

News of their approach preceded them. They passed increasing numbers of Indians and homes along the trail, and the number of dwellings increased with the passage of time. They were conversing more now.

"I am member Cherokee Tribe. I have farm, plant peach trees, raise cattle. Log cabin big enough for me and you. I make you happy."

She was silent once more, and then blurted out: "I am Anoush. I will keep you happy."

"Cherokee good people. They will like you. Soon we reach home." He smiled, and she felt good to see him less serious than he had been up to now.

They rounded a turn on the trail and suddenly were confronted by a large number of people. The Indians shook their fists and gave a shout as they came into view. They were obviously happy to see him again. He was popular. The person at the front of the crowd was dressed in full regalia complete with a headdress of many eagle feathers and colourful beaded deerskin jacket.

Eagle Claw stopped the cart in front of him and descended from the cart. The chief reached out and embraced him. Anoush didn't understand what was being said as they spoke, but the joy of their meeting was evident from their tight embrace of each other.

Eagle Claw spoke. He reached out, helped her out of the cart and brought her to the chief. She felt herself lifted off her feet. The strength of the Chief surprised her as he embraced her again.

"This my father," Eagle Claw said to her. "He pleased to see you. Will have welcome ceremony, and have welcome feast tonight."

Anoush bowed to the Chief who embraced her again. He shouted instructions to a number of braves and women and the entire camp broke into activity.

Eagle Claw took her hand and leading the horses walked to a log cabin on the outskirts of the camp. It was his home.

She was now a Cherokee. It would be formalized later at the Pow-Wow.

PART 4

CHAPTER 23

Dis-Remembering

Harold awoke with a start. It was raining heavily and the noise that woke him was thunder accompanied by flashes of lightning. It was one of those late summer storms.

He reached for his phone and dialled Sommers' number. It was still early although the sun was shining brightly as it rose over the lake. When it came over the horizon it shone directly into his bedroom and sleep became impossible. He had to get up.

"Hello," she said, "PM, I am a working lady and I need my beauty sleep. This had better be important. I'm not going to start the morning off by quarrelling with you, because if you had agreed to sleep with me here, you wouldn't have to call me."

"Honey," Harold replied, soothingly, "it is tempting to accept your offer, but this not the right time. You know me and how focused I am usually. We haven't spoken about your thesis recently, and it is important that we begin to work on this project. I'm calling you because we need to get together as soon as possible, to work seriously on it."

Sommers listened carefully.

"This is why I love you so much. You are something else. Here it is, you wake me up so early to want to talk to me about something that is so important to me. You are showing interest in my welfare to that extent?"

Harold couldn't see it, but a tear fell from her eyes. She really loved this man.

"I just feel that it is time for serious attention to the subject of your thesis. It is important. Tell me when you will meet me and get to work on it."

"We can have dinner this evening. I will be busy at work, but I'll make every effort to meet you after work. I will order some dinner from The Mandarin so that we won't have to spend any time preparing, and that will give us enough time to begin to examine my notes, references and the outline I have prepared."

"Okay," he answered. "See you later. Call me when you decide on the time. I'm going to begin some work on my computer. We'll work on this together. Don't get in any trouble in the meantime."

He hung up the telephone. She laughed out loud and then chuckled to herself. PM could be funny sometimes, she thought. He was getting old but he still had a sense of humour, a loud and infectious laugh, and even though the wrinkles in his face showed the passage of time. His warmth drew people to him.

He was her PM though, and she sometimes felt pangs of jealousy when other women were also drawn to him. As she sat at her desk she reminisced over the events that had taken place since their reunion.

Her life had become more focussed and less turbulent than a couple of months earlier. She was more settled and contented. She and Harold had become very close. They were enjoying life. PM had taken her to a number of concerts—classical and jazz at Koerner Hall, near the Royal Conservatory of Music of the University of Toronto. They had taken long walks in the many parks around the city and to a number of street fairs in the warm summer air.

Annie and Charlie were still at the reservation, but she and Sommers carried on long telephone conversations and kept abreast of each other's activities. They were to meet in another couple of weeks at Sommers' apartment to celebrate Charlie's birthday. It would be a surprise party for him. They each swore the other to secrecy, revelling in the conspiracy.

She was surprised at how easily she and 'her PM' had become almost like man and wife. She was happy. She was very much in love. Life was good.

She chastened herself and got ready for work.

It was late in the afternoon when she realized that she had not eaten any lunch. She went to a small eatery across the street had a submarine sandwich, and returned to work.

She called Harold.

"PM," she said when he answered, "don't forget we have a date this evening. You have your own vehicle now, so I will meet you at home, my home... around six thirty. As I said I will pick up some food. That will give us time to eat, and get our thoughts together before we begin work.

"All right," he answered. "I've been doing some work on the computer for the entire day. It looks as if I'm going to be employed on this project full time for a long time, so I will be expecting my pay package soon." He chuckled.

"I don't have any money," she answered, "so payment will have to be in kind, and would be subject to negotiation." She laughed loudly. "We will discuss that when we meet later."

The rest of the day passed uneventfully and then it was time to go and meet her PM. She shut down her laptop, put it in its case, called the Mandarin Chinese restaurant to order dinner, picked up her bag, and left the office.

She picked up dinner on the way home and had a quick shower. She collected her notes, tidied her desk and was ready when the telephone rang. He was on time, as usual.

His knock was barely audible. She opened the door and kissed him as he entered. She smells nice, he thought to himself as she led him to the sofa.

"PM," she said, "I'm giving you a key to this apartment so that you can let yourself in. You knocked so softly that I almost didn't hear it."

"Okay Sommers. No problem. How was your day?"

"It was great. I got a lot accomplished. Dinner is on the table. Go wash up and let's eat. I'm starving."

By the time he returned to the table she was seated and dishing out the food. They ate in silence, although Sommers kept looking at him, picking at her food, and constantly reaching across to take morsels from his plate.

"Sommers," he said in mock seriousness, "you have your food, leave mine alone."

"PM," she said just as seriously, "what's yours is mine, so I am taking what's mine." She laughed mischievously.

They finished eating, and got down to the business of the evening.

Sommers showed him her notes. She had copious references. He realized they needed proper collation, so he set about organizing them.

"You have a lot of material," he said, "but for such a complex and far-reaching study you need to set it out in categories and subcategories."

"Well PM. I thought at first that I would deal with African slavery in the U.S., but when I began my research I realized that it was not possible to deal with that in isolation. Despite what most people see on the surface as a simple matter dealing with the cruelties forced on Black people by the Whites, the Native Indians have also been subjected to much of what has been suffered by the Blacks.

"They too have been slaves... exported captured like some whites from Scotland and Ireland and sent to the Caribbean islands, made to work under the same conditions and hardships as the Blacks, and bound for life to the same cruel owners and masters.

"My research has also made the connection with the capture of, trading in, and subjecting of the Indigenous Indians of America to enslavement, slavery and the same cruelty. They worked next to the black and white slaves on the same plantations doing the same things and also suffering from similar whippings, cruelty and deprivations."

She paused. Harold was thoughtful. He twirled the pencil between his fingers.

"Continue," he said "my interest is piqued." Sommers began reading from her notes.

"Slavery of Native American Indians has been glossed over and or otherwise purposely dis-remembered. Between 1492 and 1889 between two and a half to five and a half million Native Indians were enslaved by the whites, in addition to over 12.5 million Africans. Like the blacks from Africa many had been removed from their homes and homeland and taken overseas far away. The 'rulers' of the New England colonies routinely shipped them as slaves to Barbados, Bermuda, Jamaica, and other West Indian islands, the Azores, Spain, and Tangiers in North Africa.

"The Indians who were the original inhabitants of the continent were themselves made slaves in their own land, sometimes as a result of tribal conflict. Although there was a difference in this type of slavery for they were often either assimilated into the conquering tribe, or later exchanged for their own captured people, or intermarried with members of the tribe, replacing tribesmen who had been killed or themselves captured and taken away.

"When they were captured by the whites they were exported to countries far away or made to work on plantations from which there was no escape. Fear of this fate spurred many of them to pledge to fight to the death, while many would have surrendered hoping to avoid being sent overseas.

"For colonists slavery was a normal part of their mental framework—a means of obtaining unpaid labour to maintain their lifestyle. Their opinion of the Indians was so low that in 1878 William Halley wrote in the Centennial yearbook of Alameda County, that the California Indian was "one of the most degraded of God's creatures. He was without knowledge, religion or morals, even in their most elementary forms. He lived without labor, and enjoyed all the ease and pleasure he could. Physically, he was not prepossessing, although having considerable endurance and strength. His skin was nearly as dark as that of the negro, and his hair as coarse as the hair of a horse, while his features are repulsive. To gratify his appetite and satiate his lust were his only ambition. He was too cowardly to be warlike, and did not possess that spirit of independence which is supposed to be the principal attribute of his race. In so genial a climate as ours, nature easily provided for all his wants. The best part of his time was spent dancing and sleeping.

"PM," she said quietly and scornfully, "Can you imagine a society with these attitudes toward the people whose lands they wanted to occupy? PM?"

"Yes, I can," Harold answered. "many of these attitudes still exist today and have been attached to the slaves brought over from Africa."

"Further," she added, "the introduction of Chattel Slavery put a different face to the whole aspect of slavery, these enslavement attitudes and practises permanently disrupted the lives livelihoods and kinship networks of thousands of Indians. Sometimes slavery was simply given another name."

"Shakespeare wrote that a rose by any other name smells as sweet." Harold added laconically. "Slavery by any other name is still slavery. A slave is still owned by someone."

Harold paused in his reading. He became thoughtful while drinking from his beer mug and gazing at the ceiling.

"That's why we have to divide your thesis along the lines you have outlined."

"Alright PM," Sommers said. "This is my plan of action."

Sommers explained the structure of her proposed thesis to Harold. Harold interrupted her.

"That is too much to deal with right now. Much of that has to be compressed and dealt with in a different manner. Let me think about it for a while and go through your research papers and references."

"Alright PM." Sommers answered cheerily, "you're the boss."

She kissed him lightly on his cheek and retreated to the kitchen.

"I'll continue it later."

"This plan seems alright, on the surface." Harold interjected when she returned. "We'll see how you tackle it in your writing."

Sommers handed him a number of pages. "This is a draft of what I have written so far."

She seemed nervous as he started to read. He sat

slouched in the settee, one foot on the footstool she placed for his feet, a pencil perched in one corner of his mouth, and a beer on the table next to the settee.

Harold became excited, not only by the topic, but by the direction from which Sommers was approaching it. Much of what she had written intrigued him because very little of this was taught in schools, or even discussed among academics. It was a hidden history concealed from the populace at large.

"We'll stop here for now." He said, "we'll have a full fledged discussion on it later."

"Thanks PM," she said, "I have much more in this area, so I will give you that a little later."

The phone rang. It was Annie. She seemed excited when Harold handed the receiver over to Sommers.

CHAPTER 24

Attitudes to Slavery

The attitude of the white man when he landed on the shores of the new continent was one of superiority, considering anyone else as inferior and subject to them. With the passage of time they used treaties which they broke with impunity, first through the armies they created, and abrogation of the laws they themselves created, and to which they expected everyone else to adhere.

Acts of ethnic cleansing—genocide—like those of the Indian Removal Act, the Bloody Island and Yantoket Massacres of California in which over 400 natives were killed in each massacre the killing of natives by incoming settlers, government financed and organized militias, famine, violence and starvation caused the depletion in population of native peoples from 150,000 in 1848 to just 15,000 in 1900. In addition the 1864 deportation of over 8000 Navajos to the interment camp at Bosque Redondo, where they were held under armed guard, resulted in the death of more than 3,500 Navajo and Apache men women and children.

President Theodore Roosevelt was of the opinion that the Indians were destined to vanish under the pressure of white civilization because "...I don't think that the only good Indians are dead Indians, but I believe nine out of ten are, and I shouldn't like to inquire too closely into the case of the tenth."

Resistance to expansion into Indian lands by land-hungry settlers, gold seekers and those believing in the Doctrine of Manifest Destiny—the inherent superiority of the white man and the derogation of any other in society as inferior—resulted in wars and rebellions by not only the Native Indian population, but by Blacks who resisted enslavement.

The Cherokee practice and that of many other Indian tribes prior to contact with the Europeans was to enslave their other Indian captives and assimilate them into the tribe. With the advent of African slavery, some Cherokee, following advice from some whites and emulating the 'white man's practice', established European-American and Barbadian-style plantations, and purchased African-American slaves to work the land. Following the white man's practice in 1819, established slave codes that regulated the slave trade forbade intermarriage between Blacks and Cherokee, and enumerated punishment for runaway slaves. In 1730 the Cherokee signed the Treaty of Dover with the British committing them to return runaway slaves, and prohibited Black slaves from owning private property. By 1835, the time of the Indian Removal, the Cherokee owned a total of 1,500 slaves of

African Ancestry. Within five years of removal, 300 mixed race Cherokee families made up an elite class in Indian Territory.

In 1860 the Cherokee held an estimated 4,600 slaves and depended on them as farm labourers and domestic servants. At the time of the Civil War a total of more than 8,000 slaves were held in Indian territory where they comprised 14 percent of the population.

The relationship of Africans and Indians, whether as a result of trade, capture or being rescued as runaway slaves from their white masters, resulted in large numbers of mixed race individuals.

The attitude of the new President George Washington was for "...the complete elimination of the Native Indian from the face of the earth." His instructions to the leader of the Sullivan Expedition in 1779, directed against the "hostile tribes of the Six Nations of Indians, with their associates and adherents-obviously those of mixed blood-[was] "the total destruction and devastation of their settlements and capture of as many prisoners of every age and sex possible. It was essential to ruin their crops now in the ground and prevent their planting more. He also believed that "Native American Society was inferior, he thus formulated a six point plan to 'civilize' the Indians.

The Treaty of Paris (1783) signed between the British and the United States ceded vast Native American Territory to the United States, without consulting with, or informing the Native Americans." The Creek ceded over twenty million acres of their traditional-about half of Alabama and part of Georgia. They adopted a strategy of appeasement, but neither appeasement nor resistance through warfare worked.

Even when they tried to seek justice through the courts, these decisions were ignored when it suited the leaders. The Indian Removal Act was deemed unconstitutional by the Supreme Court. This was conveniently ignored by President Jackson, who removed them through force, using the army to enforce the removal of these indian tribes, and the confiscation of their lands.

Not only were they deprived of their land, but through force of arms, Indigenous Indians were enslaved, shipped out of the country to Caribbean islands, and throughout the continent, they were subjected to ethnic cleansing.

CHAPTER 25

Opportunity

The business district of Toronto was concentrated between Yonge Street and University Avenue, encompassing City Hall, the Old Court House the new modern courts, the Stock Exchange and the major businesses within their boundaries.

Broadfoote and Broadfoote occupied an entire floor in one of the ultramodern suites of the recently constructed Toronto Dominion twin towers on King street which cut through the centre of this district. It was a large company, and very well known.

Annie occupied a corner office commanding a view from which she could observe both Yonge Street and University Avenue.

She was well liked at the firm.

When Annie answered the telephone, the voice on the other end was the head of the firm. She was summoned to an urgent meeting with him. When she entered the office, the other senior partner of the firm was with him. They motioned her to a seat opposite them. The leather chair was comfortable, but she still sat upright and on the edge.

Jim, the senior partner, began.

"Annie, you remember that we mentioned the case we are proposing to send you to Oklahoma to present. We're sending you on that trip. We've made all the arrangements. Our colleagues in the court system there have been made aware of your abilities and are prepared to be a resource for you. They will give you all the assistance you may need and will be an invaluable source of information. They will provide you with whatever you need. The case is on the docket for three weeks from today, so take as much time as you need to be prepared."

Jim's voice always made her feel comfortable. It was almost fatherly, which fooled a lot of people because he was tough as nails, and very smart. Nobody could put anything past him because he always thought quickly and was sure of what he was saying when he spoke. Annie had worked with him for a long time and she knew and respected him. She felt a surge of pride run through her.

At last they are recognizing my worth, she thought. She had always done her work thoroughly and conscientiously, contributing to the growth of the partnership and being well recommended for her appearances before the Bar, the way she dressed and her general behaviour and attitude, receiving commendations from judges and juries when she defended clients. Now she would be able to perform on a larger scale before a wider audience. This was even more satisfying when they briefed her on the case.

She was to present an appeal to the Oklahoma Supreme Court which challenged the constitutionality of a ruling by a county court on the voting rights of some Oklahomans who were descendants from Georgia Cherokees of mixed ethnicities, who were being prevented from voting. The County held that because the marriage between the parties had not been sanctified in a Christian church but in a Cherokee ceremony, and they had indicated that they were married on their voting forms, they were guilty of making false statements on their voter registration papers and thus were not eligible to vote. They further held that because it took place between a Cherokee woman and an African 'freedman', the marriage could not be accepted as legal because jumping the broom, an accepted form of marriage practised by African slaves and accepted by both Cherokee and African, was not Christian, thus the voting roles could not consider them as man and wife.

Broadfoote and Broadfoote had been retained to represent the couple in the appeals court. Annie was chosen to travel to Oklahoma to represent them in their appeal. Here was an opportunity to make the voices of the Native Indians and African-Americans heard before the entire country. She was excited about the case and accepted the opportunity to be that voice. This excitement was evident when she called Sommers and told her about it. Sommers was equally excited and they soon became submerged in preparations for the trip and the presentation of the case.

Sommers was as excited as Annie when she received

the news, and conveyed this excitement to Harold. They talked about this for a long time before they fell asleep. This case tied in with what she was doing in her preparation for her dissertation.

Annie came down from the reservation to visit with Sommers, and both she and Harold spent some time getting the spare room ready for her. Charlie remained at the reservation although he phoned her regularly.

She and Sommers set about preparing for her presentation to the Oklahoma Supreme Court.

They spent hours downtown at the Osgoode Law School of the University of Toronto researching in the Archives, examining documents, case histories and everything they could pertaining to African and Indian wedding ceremonies and practices.

Much of what they found surprised and intrigued them. One important aspect and surprise was that even the ancient Indians and Africans shared similar concepts regarding the relationships of men and women, the sacredness attached to the ceremonies, and the sincerity profoundly expressed in the ceremony.

'Jumping the Broom' was similar to ancient Irish and other ethnicities and folk customs, and was used not only as a way of getting around the restrictions placed on slaves by slave-masters, but was a sacred hallowed practice of white people. In addition, it was legal and recognized in the State legislature as long as certain procedures were followed. These had been adhered to by the couple, but the state authorities had ignored them, or were themselves not familiar with them.

This fact would form an important part of Annie's presentation. The nature of the Cherokee and African societies, where the woman was the dominant personality, a mistake the French learned to their detriment, also served to reinforce the case she was presenting.

The two of them became more immersed in the preparation for Annie's journey.

Early one morning on an extremely cold winter's day when the temperature outside was minus twenty degrees Celsius, Sommers' excited but muffled scream brought Annie from among a stack of law books. She came over.

"Look at this," Sommers said. "Here is a case: Butler vs Wilson, decided in 1915 before the Supreme Court of Oklahoma. This case, even though it is one discussing division of property among descendants of a deceased, discussed the custom of regular marriage where the marriage was entered into in accordance with the letter of the written law, or irregular, which was according to the usages and customs of the Creek Tribe or Nation, "being recognized as valid by members of the Nation and recognized as valid in the courts of the state."

"That's an interesting coincidence," Annie said just as excitedly. "I just came across a number of other interesting findings. I have a number of precedents that I can present, where it can be shown that slaves who could prove maternal descent from Native Americans were prima facie free... shows that there was a shift in leading courts to redefine natives as unfit subjects for slavery, and seeks to show the roots of the radicalization of slavery that separated Natives from Africans. It also shows that the racial ideology that divided Native Americans and Africans still poses legal problems in Indian law cases involving tribal recognition."

Their excitement grew as they unearthed more and more cases pertinent to the appeal. Annie was finally satisfied with the amount of material they had accumulated.

"Let's go home, put this material in a suitable format, and in the next couple of days I will come over and have a Moot Court. You, Charlie and PM can be the justices to whom I will make my presentation."

"That sounds really good," Sommers said. "Let's have some dinner, girl's night out, and then head home."

They indulged themselves in a lobster dinner complete with fine wine, and headed back to Scarborough.

CHAPTER 26

Appeal Broadfoote et al.

The sound of the fire truck's throaty siren as it approached an intersection followed immediately by the acceleration of the heavy engine intruded on the silence of the early morning. Traffic was light on the road.

Annie was surprised when she entered the living room. Chairs and tables had been moved around and rearranged to give the appearance of a courtroom. The dining table was the repository for books and papers, and from which the 'court clerk' and lawyers would work. It presented quite a picture. The dining chairs became the seats for the 'justices'.

She sat on the settee and placed her satchel with her notes, research papers and paraphernalia next to her. Sommers drifted in.

"Good morning Annie," she said, rubbing her eyes. "I see the men have been at work. I had no idea they were going to be so busy while we were sleeping."

"They certainly did." Annie said quietly. "It is quite a surprise. I think they want me to be successful."

"No doubt about that."

"I will certainly try very hard. This is an important assignment and will have far reaching results if I am successful."

"Let not your heart be troubled," Sommers replied, moving toward the kitchen. "You have worked hard, and you are well prepared."

"That collaboration with the firm in Oklahoma was certainly helpful. They helped a great deal with my temporary registration to present before the Supreme Court. I learned a lot from them. I am better prepared now and more comfortable and happy with my brief."

She followed Sommers into the kitchen.

"We better make a nice breakfast for our heroes. They deserve it," she said.

They busied themselves.

Charlie came into the kitchen. He went up to Annie and kissed her lightly on her cheek. He had come down from the reservation the night before. Annie had kept him up to date on her progress in preparing the appeal.

"Hi beautiful," he said, patting her on her buttocks. "I think I fall in love with you every time I see you, and especially these early mornings when you seem to glow."

He sniffed the aroma of fresh bread toasting.

"A hungry man is an angry man, so don't let me get angry. Can I have a cup of coffee?"

He reached across her and removed a cup from the dish dryer, poured coffee in it, and retreated to the living room.

"As you can see we worked very hard last night. We have a lot of work to do, and PM told me he plans to start court early, about 9.30 am, to listen to your arguments and discussion. You know he is very thorough."

Harold came into the kitchen soon after.

"Good morning Sommers," he said. He kissed her.

"Morning PM," she answered. "Your breakfast will be ready shortly."

"I'm glad to hear that. Court begins promptly at 9.30 and I expect everyone to be in their places at that time. Sommers, you will act as a justice and legal clerk, and Charlie will be acting as a justice and everything else. We will be as formal as if it were a real trial. Annie I expect you to demonstrate your skill and present your arguments cogently and succinctly."

"I understand." Annie answered.

"Let's have breakfast and then we can get down to work." He said unsmilingly.

Sommers busied herself setting the living room table with the cups, dishes, and food. They were soon silent, savouring the meal and occupied with their individual thoughts.

Harold's appearance surprised them when they had finished eating and were getting ready for Court. He appeared in his graduation robes from the university, looking everything like the serious, solemn justice of the court. He strolled in and sat in the 'high chair' with Sommers and Charlie trailing behind him.

Annie took her position. She had files and books with pages marked with coloured bits of paper. She looked almost afraid.

Sommers summoned the court to order.

"Supreme Court of Appeals, Oklahoma, 9th District. Judge Harold Watson presiding, assistant Justices Judge Sommers Blades, and Justice Charlie Deerfoot." Sommers announced. "Court is now in session." She intoned slowly and solemnly.

"Good morning all." Harold said.

"Good morning." They intoned.

"Welcome to our visiting attorney from Canada. I observe that everything is in order with regard to being temporarily licensed to practice here. We welcome you here and will hear your presentation at this time."

Annie rose.

"Honourable Justices, thanks for your welcome. I am honoured and thank you for the opportunity to present this appeal before you on behalf of Broadfoote and Broadfoote, representing the appellants Lyle and Tate."

As our brief indicates:

"From the time there was an association between males and females, there has been an innate desire for their associations to be as close as possible. Marriage became the method by which these Indians established their associations and formalized them. Before the white man came to these shores and established his own form of these associations, indigenous Indians determined the format.

"Through the establishment of slavery of Native Indians, and slavery of Africans brought over from the other side of the Atlantic, the desire for this form of association was removed from their psyche. The abolition of slavery and the constitutional amendments that followed afforded these groups the opportunity to choose their representatives by voting for them. From the time of its establishment various obstacles have been placed to deter and obstruct the free voting of those desiring to do so.

"The case before you today involves a decision of the lower court to disallow the plaintiffs to exercise their legal right to vote in the election referred to in the docket.

"The trial court has excluded the evidence that was offered. The court held that the right of the plaintiffs to vote was nullified, because their marriage was not a lawful marriage as determined by the State, that is, following a Christian format.

"It is our contention that since this marriage between a Cherokee Indian and an African American, undertaken according to the custom of their tribes and heritage, fulfils the criteria and is therefore lawful. It has been held from time immemorial that marriages between members of the tribe according to the customs of the tribe are considered valid by the tribe.

"The opinion of the Supreme Court in the case of Crabtree v Sunburn D. Madden, expressed the opinion that "the Creek Tribe of Indians is a dependent domestic nation. It is a distinct political society capable of managing its own affairs and governing itself. Marriages were either regular or irregular... regular when they complied according to the literal letter of the law, and irregular when a man and woman lived together according to the usage of the tribe as husband and wife without any compliance with the mode of ceremony according to law."

Justice Watson cleared his throat.

"I should like to know exactly where you are going with this line of argument counsel," he asked.

"I intend to establish, your honour, that the purpose of this appeal is to determine that there is no substance to the refusal of the lower court to deny the right of the plaintiffs to vote. By determining that the marriage was valid, according to the established customs of the Cherokee tribe, their appeal must be allowed.

"Jumping the broom is not only an established form of performing a marriage ceremony, but even before the white man came to these shores, a similar custom was followed in Scotland less than a century ago. Marriage by Scottish law was regular when performed by a minister of religion after the publishing of the banns or notice given by the registrar. Marriages were considered irregular, but regarded as legal when the marriage state was entered into by a simple agreement. Gretna Green became famous for irregular marriages under the Scottish Law by the simple process of jumping a broom in the presence of the blacksmith. As he stated further: 'We decline to require of the Creek people a more rigorous standard than that which governed our own ancestors. We therefore conclude that such irregular marriages among Creeks are valid... The laws of the United States and the State of Arkansas, in force in the Indian Territory, shall apply to all persons irrespective of race.

"The case before you today involves a decision of the lower court to disallow the plaintiffs to exercise their legal right to vote in the election referred to in the docket.

"The trial court has excluded the evidence that was offered. It is our contention that since this marriage between a Cherokee Indian and an African American, undertaken according to the custom of their tribes and heritage, fulfils the criteria, and is therefore lawful. It has been held from time immemorial that marriages between members of the tribe according to the customs of the tribe are considered valid by the tribe."

Justice Deerfoot interrupted at this juncture.

"We have been here a long time and I should like to request a short adjournment, for tea to be served."

"I have no objection," Justice Sommers said quietly. "I hope Justice Watson will concur."

"No objection," Justice Watson replied. "A short break of fifteen minutes should be enough."

"Court is adjourned for fifteen minutes," Justice (Court Clerk) Deerfoot said loudly.

They all rose to their feet as the 'justices' left the court.

Sommers made the coffee and served egg salad sandwiches.

Discussion was muted and Annie gathered her notes and was writing vigorously when Sommers suddenly exclaimed.

"Court is in session."

She looked up to see the 'justices' in their seats.

"Continue please, Ms. Dreamcatcher."

"Justices," she began, "having presented the

precedents and necessary legislation showing that the practice of 'jumping the broom' is a valid and accepted practice, and having established that the marriage of the plaintiffs, a Cherokee Indian and an African former slave, are also valid having been conducted according to accepted practice, the question remains to show that the denial of the ability to vote is a fundamental abrogation of their constitutional rights.

"The imposition of slavery denied the slaves, Indians and Africans, the basic rights of a person. Even though slavery removed the aspect of freedom of movement and the imposition of unpaid work, the 13th Amendment to the constitution and the Emancipation declaration removed these shackles from the slave. The passage of legislation allowing them to choose their representatives meant that the slave could now make choices.

"The attempts to undermine this right through spurious reasons and actions is a denial of the long fight for rights. There is no doubt that the authorities decided to deny the plaintiffs their constitutional rights."

"Ms. Dreamcatcher, why do you think so much emphasis should be placed on the right to vote?"

"Because, your honour, the ability to choose which master to serve is one of the distinguishing differences between slavery and freedom.

"Before emancipation the slave could not choose his master. With emancipation the slave became free to serve whomever he or she chose. The former slave would have been able to join his wife and family without interference by the authorities.

"The ability to exercise this right must not be infringed. There is no logical reason why this should not be applied here. The marriage is valid, accepted as such by the court in many cases including Butler v Martin which I referred to earlier, and since this is so, then the error of the lower court must be acknowledged. That is my presentation your honours."

"Thank you Miss Dreamcatcher. We will consider your presentation, and will inform you of the court's decision."

"Court is suspended." Justice Sommers announced as they rose and left the court.

CHAPTER 27

The Black Slave Trail of Tears

Annie and Charlie had come down to visit Sommers. The moot court justices had returned their verdict and unanimously agreed that the lower court decision should be reversed. The appeal had been successful and she was well prepared for her sojourn into the Oklahoma presentation.

They were happy with the way things were developing.

Before their return to the reservation, however, Harold had mentioned the details of Sommers' thesis to them. Annie was particularly interested. They settled in the living room, enjoying the changing colours of the trees on this Indian Summer evening.

"PM," Sommers said quietly, "Charlie told you about the ordeals of the Cherokee after the enforcement of the Indian Removal Act that forced them to take the Trail of Tears with its associated pain and suffering. However, there is another Trail of Tears, the Black Slave Trail of Tears, that has faded from the discussion of slavery, either deliberately or because it is too painful to remember. Or, more cynically, because it does not fall within the ambit or agenda of some historians." She paused.

She took a deep breath when she realized that all eyes were focussed on her.

"I never heard of this," Harold said.

"Worse than our Trail of Tears?" Charlie asked incredulously.

Sommers delved among her papers and re-emerged with a paper festooned with red markers peeping out from between the pages.

"I am quoting directly from a pamphlet issued by the Smithsonian Magazine of the Smithsonian Institution:

"The Slave Trail of Tears is a great missing migration-a thousand-mile-long-river of people, all of them black, reaching from Virginia to Louisiana. During the 50 years before the Civil War, about a million enslaved people moved from the upper south—Virginia, Maryland, Kentucky—to the deep south—Louisiana, Mississippi, Alabama. They were made to go, deported, you would say, having been sold.

This forced resettlement was 20 times larger than Andrew Jackson's Indian Removal campaign of the 1830s, which gave rise to the original Trail of Tears as it drove tribes of Native Americans out of Georgia, Mississippi, and Alabama. It was bigger than the immigration of Jews into the United States during the 19th century when some 500,000 arrived from Russia and Eastern Europe. It was bigger than the wagon train migration to the West.

This movement lasted longer and grabbed more people,

than any other migration in North America before 1900. The drama of a million individuals going so far from their homes changed the country. It gave the deep south a character it retains to this day; it changed the slaves themselves, traumatising uncountable families."

Charlie was incredulous. Annie was silent. Harold was anxious for more details.

"Continue Sommers," he said, "I'm listening."

"Franklin and Armfield," she continued, "two slave traders used to gather coffles of slaves from the Virginia countryside."

"...up and down the East Coast, knocking on doors, asking tobacco and rice planters whether they would sell any of their slaves. Many slaveholders were inclined to do so, as their plantations made smaller fortunes than many princeling sons would have liked.... It took four months to assemble a big coffle... the company's agents went down to the   slave pens in Alexandria... seeking out: seamstresses, hostlers, carpenters, cooks, houseboys, coachmen, so-called fancy girls, young women who would work mainly as concubines and always, children."

"That is incredulous," Harold exclaimed.

"There is more. The formation of the coffle, the organization and the trip itself required funding, coordination, and preparation for the long journey.

The organization of a coffle was described by witness to one of them, as described by Ethan Andrews, in 1833. "Four or five tents were spread, and the large wagons which were to accompany the expedition were stationed where they could be piled high with provisions and other necessaries. New clothes were loaded in bundles. Each negro is furnished with two entire suits from the shop.... which he does not wear on the road. Instead, these clothes were saved for the end of the trip so each slave could dress well for sale. There was a pair of carriages for the whites. In 1834 Armfield sat on his horse in front of the procession, armed with a gun and a whip. Other white men, similarly armed, were arrayed behind him. They were guarding 200 men and boys lined up in twos, their wrists handcuffed together, a chain running the length of 100 pairs of hands. Behind the men were the women and girls another hundred. They were not handcuffed, although they may have been tied with rope. Some carried small children. After the women came the big wagons—six or seven in all. They carried food, plus children too small to walk ten hours a day. Later the same wagon carried those who had collapsed and could not be roused with a whip.

Then the coffle, like a giant serpent, uncoiled onto Duke Street and marched west, out of town and into a momentous event, a blanked-out saga, an unremembered epic: The Slave Trail of Tears.

"Slave trading between different states, the internal slave trading, became an established practice. The forced migration of primarily Black slaves, often referred to as the Second Middle Passage, became an important economic factor, often mimicking the other middle passage. This era created considerable traumatising of Blacks, both slave and free, who lost connection to family and tribe—loss of tribal origin. In the mid 1800s almost 300,000 slaves were transported with Alabama and Mississippi receiving 100,000 each.

"The Indian slave trade extended from both the west and south from the south east. Slavery was part of the strategy to depopulate the land occupied by the Indians to provide land for the European settlers.

From the middle sixteen hundreds, after the Pequot war where over 300 Pequots were massacred, those who remained were sold into slavery and sent to Bermuda, passing through Boston, Salem, Mobile and New Orleans, to be sent eventually to Barbados, Martinique and Guadeloupe, and the Antilles.

"Historian Ira Berlin opined that "the internal slave trade became the largest enterprise outside the plantation itself, and probably the most advanced in the employment of modern finance, transportation, finance and publicity...

"The expansion of the interstate slave trade contributed to the revival of once depressed states, as demand accelerated the value of slaves who were subject to sale. By 1840 New Orleans had the largest slave market in North America. It became the wealthiest city in the nation, based primarily on the slave trade. In many instances Indians were not recoded in the records as

Indians, especially when they were of mixed ancestry— Indians and African intermarriage—but based on their looks, and identified by the recorders as often they were recorded, on birth certificates or plantation rolls, as black and not Indian.

As a result there is a population of people of Native

American heritage and identity who are not recognized by society at large, sharing similar circumstances with the Freedmen of the Cherokee and other five civilised tribes as determined by the Dawes Roll cards by the Dawes Roll Administration."

CHAPTER 28

Celebration

Annie interrupted Harold's perusal of Sommers' notes.

"Sommers," she blurted out. "Could you come into the kitchen with me? There is something I need to discuss with you. Something I don't want to discuss in front of these two men."

"Sure," Sommers responded. She turned to Harold. "Sorry PM, sometimes we girls have to have girl talk, alone. You have enough drinks for you and Charlie. We won't be long. Keep reading."

She kissed him lightly on his cheek. Charlie poured another beer. Sommers and Annie retreated to the kitchen.

Soon after both appeared at the entrance to the living room. They were singing. Annie was carrying a birthday cake complete with lighted candles, and Sommers was carrying a large bottle of champagne and an ice bucket full of ice.

"Happy birthday to you... happy birthday to you... Happy birthday!! Surprise!! they shouted."

Charlie was so surprised, he almost fell off the chair. Harold was just as surprised. These two women were good at keeping secrets.

Annie brought the cake to Charlie.

"Did you think I had forgotten you, my love? We didn't, and we love you very much."

She kissed him as she placed the ice and champagne on the table.

"Sommers and myself planned this secret long ago. We wanted to surprise you, this is why I came down today from the reservation."

Sommers smile was so wide she almost chocked because she really wanted to laugh out loud at the same time.

"So, PM," she said, putting the bottle of champagne into the container with ice. "Put down my papers and come and help me in the kitchen. We girls have some food prepared, we are going to eat some food, drink some drinks, and enjoy ourselves. We have a lot to celebrate and to be thankful for."

Harold complied. He put some music on the Bose system that he had helped Sommers to purchase, and the party began. They danced, ate, and enjoyed themselves thoroughly. Charlie hugged Annie tightly and even shed some tears. Sommers felt as if she would cry also, but she was so tipsy that all she could do was to hold on to Harold with her head on his shoulder.

She really didn't want to let him go.

They were sleeping by the time the sun rose over the lake. They had simply collapsed from tiredness and inebriation wherever they had been sitting. There was no need to move. It was easier to close eyes and go to sleep.

Continuation of the discussion on slave rebellions didn't begin until the afternoon, By then the dishes had been washed, empty bottles and cans had been placed in the containers for recycling, and the apartment tidied up. Annie and Sommers were happy. It had been a good night that they thoroughly enjoyed. Charlie could hardly wipe the grin off his lips. He kept bothering Annie in the kitchen. She even tried to complain to Sommers.

"Sommers, will you ask this man to leave me alone?" she said half seriously.

"I am not getting between you two lovers." Somers said equally seriously, "But he is right, you are the one who presented him with a cake and plied him with drinks all night long. He is just happy."

"A girl can't even depend on her friend to come to her rescue when she is under attack." She stuck her tongue out at Charlie who promptly pulled at her locks, and ran into the living room. Annie squealed with laughter, running after him.

Harold was all business later in the afternoon after they had eaten leftovers from the night before. He announced that he was ready to continue the discussion.

"Slave driver!" was Sommers comment.

They all burst out laughing. The giddiness from the

night before seemed to have taken over. Annie couldn't stop laughing.

"Seriously folks, let's get down to Brass-tacks!" Harold continued.

Sommers then had to explain to Annie and Charlie, that Brass-Tacks was a popular call-in show on Barbadian radio. They settled down.

"Let's start off by looking at a few of the rebellions that Sommers is working on. Let's look at the Seminole Rebellion,"

He continued.

"The Black Seminoles-Freedom fighters of Oklahoma and Florida created the largest slave rebellion in the country's history.

As early as 1684 escaping African slaves, fleeing from South Carolina Low Country, seeking freedom, they travelled to Spanish Florida. There they joined Native Seminoles, who integrated with them and became part of the wider Seminole Nation."

"The Black Seminoles, descendants of Maroons— derived from the Spanish word for runaway escaped slaves—built their own settlements and adopted their own 'culture' speaking Gullah, a mixture of Afro-English creole language, and adopting an African leadership structure. They formed alliances with Creek and other Indian tribes and joined in the struggles against the encroachment in and occupation by the White man of Indian lands.

"Andrew Jackson's Indian Removal Act, which

included the Seminoles in its net, greatly affected the Black Seminoles along with other Indian tribes. Over 4,000 Seminoles including 800 Black Seminoles joined the other tribes like the Cherokee who travelled along the Trail of Tears. Many of the Black Seminoles who went on that trip never returned. The Black Seminoles understood that if the native Seminoles had to go on that trail, failure to go with them might have resulted in being forced back into slavery as a result. They joined forces with the militant Native Seminoles under the leadership of Osceola in revolt, and fought against the U.S. Army.

"From the winter of 1835 to the summer of 1836, the Black Seminoles and escaped African slaves, whom they recruited from various plantations, fought together destroying sugar plantations. It is estimated that they destroyed over 21 sugar plantations during their war against the U.S. Army.

"The U.S. government sought to turn the Black Seminoles against the Native Seminoles by offering freedom in return for their betrayal. Very few took up the offer.

"The struggles were so fierce and the army found it so difficult to completely defeat the alliance of the Native Seminoles and the Black Seminoles, that after three years of fighting the army chose to offer them freedom in return for surrender. This was the only emancipation of rebellious African Americans prior to the Civil War.

After their surrender, many Black Seminoles migrated to the Bahamas or to Mexico.

"The Black Seminoles fought and died for their freedom, a battle that continues up to today. Since the 1930s the Seminole Freedmen, descendants of the original travellers on the Trail of Tears, have struggled with the cycles of exclusion from the Seminole Nation of Oklahoma. In the 1990s the tribe received the majority of a 46 million dollar judgement Trust by the United States government for seizure of lands in Florida in 1823, and the Freedmen have worked to gain a share of it.

"From 1835-1838 the Black Seminoles and their African Slave allies, assisted by African Slaves from plantations in the area, led the largest slave rebellion in U.S. history. Scholars pay almost no attention to the role the plantation slaves played in this rebellion. They downplay all incidents of slave resistance as if they never occurred or were of any importance.

Historians chose to achieve the goal of "helping forget the South's defeat at the hands of Black rebels," by glossing over the role of the plantation slaves revolts.

"Bringing it closer to home," he continued, "along the same vein we have to consider the Bussa rebellion in Barbados."

Before the Bussa Rebellion in 1815, Bussa, who was sometimes referred to as Bussoe, was captured in Africa and brought to Barbados as a slave. Even though details of his life are recorded in historical documents, much is not revealed of his early life. The first records of his life indicate that he was a Ranger, a head officer among the enslaved workers, which gave him a degree of freedom of movement throughout the area at Bayley's plantation in St. Philip. Bussa planned the uprising in collaboration with slaves at other plantations.

In the 124 years after its settlement, the rebellion in Barbados, led by Bussa, was the first revolt by African slaves against the establishment. He and fellow conspirators including Nanny Grigg who was literate and worked at Simmons Plantation, helped plot and coordinate the rebellion that followed. About 400 slaves were successfully recruited and followed Nanny's exhortation that 'the only way to obtain freedom is to fight for it'.

"The planters leading the country had rejected an Imperial Registry Bill in November 1815, following the call for the abolition of slavery some time before. In 1807 the British Parliament had passed the act to end the slave trade. In 1815, when Governor Leith returned from Guadeloupe, the slaves thought that he was bringing a paper that would set them free. This was not the case, and it precipitated the dissatisfaction that caused the plotting for the overthrow of the system to begin.

"The Rebellion, planned over a number of weeks before the Easter Sunday when it began, was supported by the slaves at almost all the plantations in the island, although the start of the struggle took place at Bayley's Plantation, a cane fire being the signal to the rest of the country that the Rebellion had begun.

"It began on Easter Sunday. The signal would be the lighting of cane fires. The plantation owners panicked when they realised the extent of the revolt. Martial Law was declared, and the militia, the First West Indies Regiment, an all Black regiment of the British Army, became involved. This uprising where the enslaved and the planters and militia were in conflict with each other was the most significant in the history of the island.

"The superior arms of the militia caused the defeat of the Rebellion and the death of Bussa, but it resulted in a change in the political and social atmosphere of the country. The battle continued for three days. In the end 50 slaves died in the fighting and 70 died in the field. Three hundred were taken to Bridgetown for trial, 144 were executed, and 132 sent to another island.

"Bussa became a symbol of the right to live in freedom, and the Emancipation statue, actually sculpted by Guyanese-Barbadian artist, Karl Broodhagen, was commissioned to commemorate Emancipation for the slaves. Over time it has been associated with Bussa and the fight for freedom."

Sommers stopped speaking.

"You know, PM," she said sombrely, "Sometimes I get discouraged at the mass of historical data there is about the Indigenous Indian slavery and enslavement. Enough is not taught of these episodes."

"I know Sommers," Harold said, "After all you have taught me, because you are now my teacher, I feel that we all have a job to do, to which we have to dedicate ourselves. We have to recall this disremembered history and bring it to the memory of those yet to learn about it."

CHAPTER 29

Slavery in Barbados and Bermuda

Harold led off the discussion when they had settled, after lunch.

"Let's look at the issue of slavery in Barbados and Bermuda, and compare and contrast these two systems.' Sommers, let's see what you have on this aspect."

"Alright PM, this is what I have so far."

She handed him a sheath of papers .

"What do you think?"

He read:

"Slavery in Barbados and Bermuda; two islands many miles apart, but settled around the same time. Barbados: first discovered by the Portuguese, in the early 1600s, but left uninhabited; except by a few hogs left for their next visit."

"Barbados was later visited and settled by the English, who claimed the island for England; leaving a marker: "James, King of E, and of this Island in Jamestown (Holetown)."

Each island instituted the system of Involuntary Servitude, around the same time, but each differed in the initial institution of the system.

In Bermuda there was a transformation from indentured servitude to slavery—life servitude. In the early years of the country's establishment, Blacks and Indians were not slaves, but Indentured servants.

When Bermuda needed a work force slavery was legalized. The conditions of slaves were shaped primarily by the tobacco culture. Its structure and composition were not conducive to large scale agricultural production. Absence of soil conditions conducive to the growth of sugar cane, and the accompanying plantation type labor differed from that of Barbados and other islands. In the absence of this type of structure associated with the growth of sugar cane due to the growth of tobacco, the growth of the maritime revolution and the 'specialization' of pearl divers and tobacco planters meant that the need for brawn was not a necessity for importation of large numbers of African or Indian slaves.

Watson points out that "the dynamics of the Barbadian population varied significantly from those of other English colonies in the Caribbean islands." In addition, the Black population reproduced itself ...to the extent that rather than have to depend on imported blacks, they were able to satisfy the labor requirements from within.

"The Black population also had characteristics which were different from those of the other islands. The high percentage of creole-born Blacks as opposed to Africans contributed to the early development of a Barbadian identity. In addition Barbados was the only one of the British islands which supported the act abolishing the slave trade. However, the slave trade was important for the economy of the island. Because of its geographic location, it served as a re-exporting facility for slaves to the Americas and other Caribbean islands.

"The picture in relation to Barbados in the 17th and 18th centuries is one of rapid change after settlement where within a short time, based on the unfree labor of large numbers of Africans for the production of sugar, the island became wealthy, and the port of Bridgetown became a busy trading hub.

"Barbados was a stable, mature slave society, tightly controlled by its resident native white elite class with functioning institutions of its own and a specific character and identity which stamped it as undeniably and uniquely Barbadian.

"Unlike Barbados, Bermuda was settled when the vessel Sea Venture, owned by the English Virginia Company, established in Jamestown, Virginia, was wrecked on a reef in 1609. To prevent its sinking the sailors deliberately scuttled the ship and settled on the island. The island was administered as an extension of Virginia by the company until 1614. The Somers Isles Company took over in 1615 and managed the company until in 1684 when the company's charter was revoked.

The population of Bermuda which, after the English Civil War, consisted of emigrant families bound for 4-5 years as tenant farmers, paying for their rental of land, paying this rent from the proceeds of the tobacco grown. Indentured servants, serving for five years indentureship in return for passage, reduced the need for slaves in growing tobacco and provision. There was no need therefore for the active importation of African and Indian slaves; it depended instead on those captured by privateers, then sold in Bermuda. The importance of indentured servants ceased around the 1690s when the island moved to a system of 'involuntary servitude' (slavery) and a maritime economy which incorporated slave sailors, carpenters, coopers, blacksmiths, masons and shipwrights. These were hired out by their owners with the slave being paid wages with two thirds of these wages being paid to the owners.

"Slaves could be obtained by sale or purchase for auction debt, legal seizure, or by deed of gift. Revolts by slaves at various times between 1664 and 1674, overthrown with the execution of perpetrators, resulted in the 1674 Act mandating that "slaves straying from their premises, wandering at night without permission or gatherings of 2-3 slaves from different tribes, could result in whippings. Any blacks deemed free were required to become slaves again or leave the island. The importation of additional slaves were also banned.

"Slavery in Barbados and Bermuda developed along completely different lines. While Barbados became one of the major hubs in the development of African slavery, the Trade Winds facilitating the voyage from Africa to the West Indies and America, it was also very instrumental in perpetuating and facilitating its spread into North

America, codifying and perfecting the control of these slaves through the slave codes adopted by South Carolina, almost verbatim from the Barbados slave codes.

"These attitudes contributed to the development of the lifestyle of the American South and eventually led to the American Civil War.

"In Bermuda, through the indentureship system and being subject to less involuntary servitude through the granting of opportunities for their slaves to earn wages, differences in the lifestyles and attitudes of the populace existed.

"Bermuda used Black sailors to develop their maritime development. During the American War of Independence, American privateers were surprised to see Bermudian privateers with Black crews among the sailors. Bermuda had legislated that part of all its sailing ships "must be made to include Blacks".

"When the Bermudian privateer Regulator was captured, it was found that almost all of the crew were Black slaves. Authorities in Boston offered them their freedom, but all 70 elected to be treated as Prisoners of War. When they were sent to New York on the sloop Duxbury, they seized the vessel and sailed it back to Bermuda. During the war of 1812, Bermudian privateering and naval vessels captured 298 ships. Black crews on Bermudian vessels showed they were as good as or better than any others sailing at that time.

"Slaves in Bermuda were acquired through purchase from other West Indian islands, Central America and

Africa, through slave markets in these places. Barbados and St. Thomas were among the main suppliers of African slaves while Indians were sent from New England, Central America and other West Indian islands. When they were imported directly, they were usually put on the auction block, although in some instances the purchase was for the Somers Island Company who became owned by the company, or in some cases private individuals, or His Majesty's Government.

"Those owned by the Company operated from a pool, and were drawn on to meet various needs. They could also be 'leased' to individuals, officers of the Company or government officials for specific periods of time. This applied to both Black and Indian slaves. This leasing of slaves for specific times, sometimes stretching into their old age, presented problems for Company slaves and in some cases when they were owned by individuals. Private individuals could own as many Black and Indian slaves as they could afford. They used their Black slaves first as indentured servants, but according to Backwood, with "the shift to perpetual servitude, they saw the advantages in Blacks whose colour made them easily identifiable and who could be disciplined with impunity, since they were not Christians, and the supply of them seemed inexhaustible.

"Private individuals who saw these advantages got involved early in owning and selling Blacks and Indians. A slave was often owned by many masters in succession. He could be sold suddenly and without warning to the slave master. A depressed economic situation could prompt the owner to sell slaves, since they were primarily an economic investment.

"Bermuda's slave ownership ended with the Emancipation declaration and the passage of a bill in the general Assembly manumitting their slavery, offering compensation to their owners and the institution of the apprenticeship system.

"With the introduction of sugar cane farming by the Dutch in 1842 and the production of sugar, Barbados soon was able to use this new source of revenue to become one of the wealthiest Caribbean islands with a labor force through African enslavement, and another port to which Indian slaves, captured in wars or otherwise, could be exported.

"The sociological changes that took place through the development of a plantocracy—wealthy planters to the exclusion of poor whites-and non-whites from the political system. [[this is not a sentence]] The needs of the sugar plantations that required a large labor force and the constant importation of slave labor resulted in Barbados becoming one of the leaders in the slave trade from European colonies. By the early 1800s the majority population shifted from a majority white to a majority Black population profile.

"The small planter elite who "held the best land, sold the most sugar, and monopolized the best offices, meant that in only one generation the planters had turned this small island into an amazingly effective sugar production machine and had built a social structure to rival the tradition-encrusted hierarchy of old England.

"Fear of rebellions and uncertainty of their place in the political and sociological place in the island, the White indentured servants and the plantation owners sought to leave the island.

"This fear was justified, for between 1649 and 1692 there were three slave rebellions (1649, 1675, 1692,) which were all successfully defused and subdued. These did not defeat the desire for freedom among the slaves and in 1816 the Easter Rebellion—the Bussa Rebellion—in which the slaves fought for three days against the organized militia of the island's regiment—with the destruction of many plantations and the burning of sugar cane fields—which resulted in the eventual defeat of the rebelling slaves despite the loss of life among the slaves through capture and execution did have far reaching consequences.

"The island, because of this Rebellion, the largest ever taking place in the history of the island, resulted in changes to the 'Consolidated Slave Law' legislation (The Emancipation Act) which gave the slaves the right to own property, the right to testify in all court cases, and reduction in fees charged for Manumission.

"According to the 1838 Master and Servants Act, discrimination against persons of colour in Barbados became illegal. However, the earlier introduction of the Apprenticeships for freed slaves working as indentured servants under labor contracts that did not allow them to enter the educational systems and labour contracts were for 12 years. These indentured servants worked as long as 45 hours a week without pay in exchange for accommodation in tiny huts, and were also paid the lowest wages in the region.

"Both Barbados and Bermuda, despite having different systems of slavery, still played important roles in the slave trade and slavery and its spread throughout the Americas.

"Slaves imported into Bermuda from other West Indian islands, Central America and Africa, may have become indentured servants. In the early years of the 17th century, Barbados and St. Thomas were the main sources of Bermuda's slave supply.

"Packwood indicates that Bermuda "in the 17th century traded for slaves with the Spaniards... the records do not show many slave ships arriving ...directly from Africa... although two actually sailed to Africa for the sole purpose of securing slaves (going to catch blackbirds).

"Many slaves—Blacks and Indians—imported into Bermuda were owned by the Somers company (company slaves), the government (King's slaves), slaves who were annexed from the Somers company, or private individuals who could own as many slaves as they could afford until limits were imposed. They used their first Blacks as indentured servants, but with the shift to perpetual servitude, they saw the advantages in blacks whose colour made them easily identifiable, and who could be disciplined with impunity as they were not Christians and the supply of them could be inexhaustible.

Charlie intruded on their thoughts.

"Annie we have to bid these folks goodbye for now. We have to go home. You will be leaving for Oklahoma shortly and we have to make final preparations."

"Yes honey," Annie replied quietly. "You have to do the driving. I am too tired to handle it at this time."

"No problem," he said.

They left the apartment soon after, Sommers seeing them to the door. Harold waved goodbye to them.

CHAPTER 30

The Court

Annie came to see Sommers and Harold before going to the airport to take her flight to Oklahoma. Her preparations for the case were complete. The representatives from the law firm in Oklahoma would meet her at the airport when she arrived and would guide her in her presentation.

They were in a long thoughtful, quiet discussion before they went to bed.

"Are you feeling alright?" Sommers asked her. Harold was quietly working at his computer.

"I am a bit nervous," Annie said. "There is a lot riding on my performance."

"I'm sure you will do alright."

"I'm not worried about my research, but even though I read up on the backgrounds of the justices, I am still conscious of the fact that I am Indian, and the prejudices in this country still run deep."

"You did your research thoroughly, and all you have to do is speak from your heart."

Sommers reached across the distance between them

and hugged her.

"Thanks," Annie said. "I'm glad I came here before I leave on that journey."

"Our thoughts and prayers will be with you. You will not be alone." Sommers said quietly and comfortingly.

She left Annie to her thoughts while she went into the kitchen to prepare coffee for all of them.

The flight to Oklahoma was uneventful. She slept most of the way there. Her company was there when she arrived and passed through the terminal.

Hal, the senior member of the firm, was tall, muscular and handsome. His grip when he shook her hand was warm and conveyed strength. He introduced her to Hazel, a middle-aged, stocky woman with a ruddy complexion. She was motherly and made Annie feel like she would be good at baking pies. She was down to earth. They took her to the hotel and stayed long enough to have a cup of coffee with her, discussing their arrangements for taking her to the courthouse the next morning, and going over her notes and the brief, offering suggestions and advice. They seemed quite pleased with her thoughts on the presentation.

She settled in her room, and kicking off her shoes, lay on the bed intending to be completely relaxed before dinner. The apple blossoms on the trees outside her window could be seen through the light curtains. It was peaceful.

The courtroom was silent. A slight breeze ruffled the dark curtains behind the chairs on the raised dais before the desks, tables with computers, and the Law books with coloured paper marking passages in them. A small number of visitors were steadily coming into the room.

Annie and the Oklahomans from the associated law firm, her supporting resource team, were in quiet conversation. They discussed the strategy they would use in making her presentation, and periodically checked some of her references. She was confident. She had prepared well.

The court clerks entered and set about preparations for the commencement of proceedings. The three justices, looking alert and dressed in their black robes, took their seats. Court was in session.

The court clerk outlined the details of the court case.

"Appeal of case Number 00015, appeal against the findings of the county court re Restriction on ability of plaintiff to vote in a general election because of an unlawful marriage. Annie Dreamcatcher, of the Firm of Broadfoote and Broadfoote of Toronto in the Province of Ontario, Canada advocating on behalf of the appellants.

The requisite legal hurdles having been cleared, and Miss Dreamcatcher, having satisfied the legal requirements to practice in the State of Oklahoma to function on behalf of the plaintiffs, the case is cleared for adjudication by the Supreme Court of Oklahoma."

The Chief justice cleared his throat.

"Miss Dreamcatcher, we have read your brief and will hear your presentation at this time. Let us welcome you to the State of Oklahoma, and we look forward to your presentation."

Annie rose and approached the podium.

"Let me thank your honour for his welcome, on behalf of the other justices and through you the lovely State of Oklahoma. As a visitor to your country, and especially this state, I am honoured to appear before you."

Her knees, which had trembled when she first got up, were more steady now and with the passage of time she became more sure of herself and calmer. Her heart rate decreased. She warmed to her task.

"Justices, the importance of this case cannot be over-emphasised. It is of significance because it impinges on A, history—the history of the era of slavery, B, the laws of nature—the intimate relationship of human interaction determined by the laws of nature, C, the laws laid down by the constitution of the United States that govern our actions, and D, the abrogation of rights guaranteed under the 15th Amendment to the constitution of the United States.

The Justices were listening intently, their gaze focussed on her.

"In the early history of this country, and in response to the concept that slaves could not legally marry, for to fasten upon a master of a female slave, a vicious, corrupting negro, sowing discord, and dissatisfaction among all his slaves, or else a thief, or a cut-throat, and to provide no relief against such a nui- sance, would be to make the holding of slaves a curse to the master."

The Chief Justice interrupted.

"Are you saying, Miss Dreamcatcher, that this was an opinion of the society at large?"

The other justices looked at her implicitly.

"Your honour," she answered calmly, "this was the opinion of nearly all white people in a society that restrained the freedom of the Black and Indian segment of the society, and kept them as slaves."

"Continue." He said.

"During the nineteenth century, the law sought to give new definition to family life, proscribing the roles of husband and wife, setting the parameters of marriage and divorce, and adjusting ancient rules and taboos about sex and procreation outside of marriage.

"The body of law that emerged recognised the family as an organic, autonomous legal entity, and established the framework for the public governance of private life still remaining to this day. Laws were introduced, manipulated and adjusted to reflect values which in themselves were against the laws of nature.

"The slave family, however, was constructed outside of legal developments governing family relationships. The notion of legal autonomy within the private sphere had no meaning for the slave family, whose members could lawfully be spread to the four corners of the slave south.

"Notwithstanding blood ties and romantic love, the slave family could not be an organic unit of permanently linked, interdependent persons. In the eyes of the law, each slave stood as an individual unit of property, and never as a submerged partner in a marriage or family. The most universal life events— marriage, procreation, child rearing—were manipulated to meet the demands of the commercial enterprise. Although slaves did marry, procreate, and form families, in some cases even under the compulsion of the master, they did so without the sanction of southern law.

"The abolition of slavery also meant the abolition of the master's control of the lives of his property. The slave could now be joined in matrimony legally. This, however provided for a conundrum.

"Thus the slave was, from a legal perspective, at once a person and a thing. The implications of the slave's dual status because the law of the family was difficult to untangle, for there was an analogous duality in family law itself [[this is not a sentence]]. Marriage, for example, legally changed both social and property relations because parenting itself created new social and property relations. The law favored and protected family relationships and sought to regulate these social relations using, among other legal tools, criminal sanctions. Therefore, if the criminal law was properly an instrument of social control for both slave and non-slave alike, how could its inapplicability to slave sexual morality be explained?

"The hybrid nature of family relationships such as marriage was the source of the problem. As the slave was a moral and social being, the strictures of legal marriage logically should have been applied to him or her. But the slave was a chattel, and therefore as legal marriage altered property relations for the new husband and wife, the law of marriage had no meaning for the slave.

"Of importance to this case, however, is consideration of the replacement of physical punishment for not adhering to the Christian format, for being wedded, by a moral code that determined the legality of the union. In this case before you, the State has abrogated to itself to punish the citizens who did not adhere to this format.

"The plaintiffs, following the customs adopted by their individual tribal customs—Cherokee and African—decided to sanctify their union by jumping the broom. The State has determined that this format is not accepted practice among Christian adherents, and negated their attempt to exercise their Constitutional right to vote in an election, declaring their marriage null and void."

She paused and took a sip from the glass of water on the podium, and the silence became louder. The fan from the air conditioner needed balancing.

She glanced at her compatriots and obtained a reassuring nod and a smile form Hal. She continued.

"Gentlemen, the attempts to impose laws, rules and regulations to the relationship between male and female amplifies the impossibility of a legal marriage, where society puts limits on this relationship. In addition, and the most important aspect of this case is the denial of the plaintiffs their constitutional right to vote in an election, solely on the basis of an interpretation of these impossible laws. The right to vote in an election is guaranteed in the constitution, and shall not be denied on the whim of officials who adhere strictly to Christian dogma.

Jumping the Broom has been shown and accepted as legal and legitimate, and as a consequence it is our submission that the appeal against the State's decision should be accepted and their decision reversed.

"I thank your honours for your patience and your permission to make this presentation."

She bowed to the Justices and sat.

"Thank you Miss Dreamcatcher. We will consider your presentation and you will be duly informed."

They rose from their seats and trooped out of the courtroom.

She felt drained. Hal and the other compatriots showed their enthusiasm by the energy they displayed in shaking her hands and congratulating her.

CHAPTER 31

The Question of Reparations

It was a beautiful Indian summer evening with the kaleidoscope of colours painted by the changing leaves.

"Sommers," Harold said to Annie and Charlie as they sat on her balcony, "is making great progress in her discussion of the contents of her thesis. I have been able to provide some input."

"Don't mind him," Sommers interrupted, "he has been invaluable in the direction in which he is guiding me. His input has been of immense help. I am so fortunate to have his wisdom, guidance and help."

"I can only provide guidance and suggestions, she provides, as the old people would say, the meat on the bones. I'm glad the two of you have come to see us again. I am going to call on both of you to provide some in-depth analysis of things from an Indian perspective, especially in the area of Reparations for the Indians.

"There is lots of discussion in the Caribbean on the need for payment to Africans who were kept as slaves, for the imposition of their enslavement. Actually there is a world-wide movement toward it.

"The Caribbean has been pushing strenuously for the payment of Reparations from the British for the benefits they derived from enslavement of Africans, who provided the major labour force for the plantation economy that provided the wealth of the British gentry. However, although the subject of Reparations has been discussed somewhat in the United States, there has been no serious discussion of Reparations to the Native Indigenous peoples for what they have suffered over the centuries."

He paused.

"Even though Europeans, French, Dutch, and British found Native Indians on the continent when they landed in the 17th century, it was not until after 1817 that the Cherokee became the first Native Americans recognized as U.S. citizens. Under Article 8 of the 1817 Cherokee Treaty, "upward of 300 Cherokees (Heads of Families) in the honest simplicity of their souls, made an election to become American citizens... In 1871, Congress added a rider to the Indian Appropriations Act... ending United States recognition of additional Native Tribes or Independent Nations and prohibiting additional treaties."

"You know," Annie said, with furrowed brow. She had been showing extreme interest when Harold indicated how far Sommers had reached in her writing, and had read much of it to them. "I've been thinking a lot on this subject. It is as if no one thinks of us, the indigenous Indian people. We have faded from the consciousness of the majority of the people of country. The denial of native identity is demonstrated by our exclusion from the reins of power, and the actual governing of the country, a country that was ours first.

"Even today we Senecas are denied our rights, rights we never ceded to the government over the years, and even where there were leases, when at the expiry of these leases we seek to exercise our rights, we are treated as if we are doing them a wrong in seeking those rights. All we are seeking is Justice. Author David Grann records this injustice in his book: Killers of the Flower Moon where he writes of the murders committed by white men against the Osages, simply to get at their money.

"The Osages, at one time, became some of the richest people on the planet. The Indian Removal Act and encroachment by White settlers had forced them onto a small area of Oklahoma unsuited to agriculture, making it very difficult for them to even feed themselves.

"Then oil was discovered on their reservation. Suddenly these Indians became extremely wealthy. In negotiating the treaty that gave them the land on the reservation, they had written in the conditions that they would retain the rights to anything found under the land, thus giving them the mineral rights to the oil. In addition, the matrilineal society that existed among them meant that the women controlled the succession of inheritance. In an attempt to get control of this oil wealth, many white men married Osage Indian women, and then plotted and carried out the plans, to kill the women they had married so as to inherit their property, and in addition murdered many other Osages. These Osage were murdered just for their wealth.

"Grann's book details how the solving of these Osage murders led to the formation of the modern FBI, the Federal Bureau of Investigations."

"Very true, and interesting, Annie," Harold responded. "We too, as Black people, against whom unspeakable wrongs have been committed, are seeking justice. But while there is no doubt that the White man, whether English, French Dutch or otherwise, can be easily found guilty on moral grounds for these violations of human rights, can a provable case be made out for the payment of reparations and a remedy sought, in the type of reparations that would satisfy these remedies?

"I have difficulty getting this aspect sorted out in my own mind. As a former leader of a government, I know the thinking that has to go into formulating these remedies, taking into consideration the length of time that has passed since the time when these atrocities were committed, and now I understand what has to be considered in terms of the thinking of those not directly affected. What would be the thinking of white people who have not been affected in any way? What would but the thinking of those of mixed race, whether Afro-Indian, Indian, White, Afro-White, or any other admixture, but who have been also subject to the same condition?

"What about the form of the reparations? What sorts of reparations? How should it be paid? Can it be enforced in any way? How? With whom should or would the case or cases be processed against? Who would be involved? Would there be Government involvement? Who would be involved in any negotiations? Would any decision negotiated and reached be legally enforceable and binding? Given the length of time that has passed, who would qualify to give evidence at any potential trial?

"Cornelius Holmes, a former slave, once said: Though the slavery question is settled, its impact is not. The question will be with us always. It is in our politics, our courts, on our highways, in our manner, and in our thoughts, all day every day.

"What about today? Is there actually provable physical or psychological hurt, or as occurred in the Salem Witch Trials, collective hysteria at the events even though the events happened hundreds of years ago. And this applies to all people who have been subjected to enslavement and suffered the inhumanity of slavery.

"In a discussion on America's moral Debt to African Americans, founding director of the National Museum of African Americans Lonnie Bunch wonders how a nation repays a moral debt, and suggests a number of ways: education, affordable health care, and neighbourhoods that are safe.

"Caribbean citizens of African descent—themselves the dropped fruit from the trees of slavery—whose involuntary servitude and unpaid labor built the bastions upon which today's civilizations stand, are the beneficiaries of this unpaid for labor, although as in the case of Bermuda, slaves were paid to some extent. Scholars of these same societies, wherein the roots are planted, also wrestle with this problem.

"To this end commissions have been formed and a Caribbean Ten Point plan has been formulated to address this matter.

The major points of this plan are:

European Governments were the owners of enslaved Africans instructed genocidal actions upon indigenous communities.

Created the legs, financial and fiscal policies necessary for the enslavement of Africans

Defined and enforced African enslavement as in their national interests

Refused compensation to the enslaved with the ending of their enslavement

Compensated slave owners at emancipation for the loss of legal property rights in enslaved Africans

Imposed a further one hundred years of racial apartheid upon the emancipated

Imposed for another one hundred years policies designed to perpetuate suffering upon the emancipated and survivors of genocide

And have refused to acknowledge such crimes or to compensate victims and their descendants."

"Do you think I should deal with this subject in any depth, PM?" Sommers asked earnestly.

"To be truthful," he answered, "I've been thinking of this a lot. It might be better to discuss this at length as part of post-graduate study. There is a lot to be covered in such a topic and a lot more research would have to be done and discussion sought over the legal cases to be made out for reparations. I don't think you have the right material now to do justice to that aspect, especially since modern slavery, in its many aspects, would have to be considered as part of the discussion. The situation of refugees from national conflicts where people have to flee from the fighting, become refugees, and because of economic conditions, starvation and inbuilt prejudice and racism, succumb to the same conditions that caused the slavery and enslavement that existed in the seventeenth and eighteenth centuries.

"In addition there are many contrary opinions being propounded by researchers employing newer methods of defining ancestry and are making claims, such as Dane Calloway who maintains that Indians were captured, sent to Europe, exchanged for resources in Africa, and shipped back to North America as Africans. The indigenous people of the Americas, the Aborigines, are among the most unique in all of the world.

"Calloway explains that for two decades researchers have been using a growing volume of genetic data to determine whether ancestors of Native Aborigines emigrated to the New World in one wave or successive waves, or from one ancestral population or a number of different populations... an international team of scientists thinks it can put the matter to rest. Virtually without exception, the new evidence supports the single ancestral population theory.

"Even today we have women being made sex slaves by one way or another, taken advantage of, and being sold into slavery and all sorts of depravity.What about Reparations and Justice for them?"

CHAPTER 32

Return to Paradise

He was seated at the long table in the coffee shop in the mall where many of his friends gathered to exchange news and gossip of home. The coffee was good, freshly brewed, and the coconut covered donut was tasty. Time was passing slowly and he enjoyed this time alone, before any of the others came, to think back on all that transpired since he left his home country. Each one of them lived back home vicariously. It was how they connected with each other and where their navel strings were buried.

Life was good, and he was enjoying it.

The voice came from directly behind him. He was startled. He froze. He knew it too well.

"Hello Harold," it said.

The mellifluous honey-dripping tones were unmistakable, although the delivery was different. The enunciation was slower than he had heard before. It was deeper, more local in accent.

Mildred! His heartbeat increased.

He turned and looked at her. His eyes opened wide,

and his mouth fell open. It was indeed Mildred, but she had changed drastically. Her cheeks had shrunken and the grey hair, showing beneath the scarf that covered her head, made her look much older than he knew she was.

He tensed.

"Hello Mildred," he said tersely. It was difficult to formulate the words.

She was not the stylish and fastidious person he knew in the past. She was drab. There was no style in what she was wearing. She looked as if she had dressed hurriedly, with whatever she could find to wear. She used to spend lots of time preparing to go out.

He was dumbfounded. Was this the Mildred that he was wedded to formerly? The wife of the Prime Minister? Who drove a stylish car, had a well and tastefully furnished office, and kept bonsai carefully nurtured, in that office? Memories came back in a split second.

He hesitated.

"Well are you going to offer me a coffee? Aren't you going to invite me to sit?" she said.

She didn't wait for his answer. She moved the stool from the space in front of him, placed the oversized bag hanging from her shoulder in the other stool, and sat with her elbows on the table top. She was waiting for him to do something; to say something.

Anger boiled in him at her presumption. He was tempted to just walk away. But then the calmness that had come to him during his weeks of confinement and months of introspection caused by his illness, took over. He had learned self control.

"What would you like?" he asked quietly, almost resignedly.

"Black coffee, no sugar, and an old-fashioned plain donut."

He walked slowly to the counter and stood in the short line. A maelstrom of emotions passed through his brain while he waited to be served. He looked back at the table. She seemed deep in thought, looking straight ahead.

What the hell is she doing here? How did she find me? Why has she chosen to come into my life again?

Not that she was coming back into his life again. That episode, that phase, had come and gone and there was no going back, whatever the reason. There was also trepidation, and he looked around the corner of the food court's entrance. He expected the others to begin arriving at any moment, and he also expected Sommers to join him. He was startled when the voice behind the counter intruded on his thoughts.

"Oh, I'm sorry," he said quickly to the petite Sri Lankan serving the customers, "I'd like a small black coffee and an old fashioned plain donut."

"Thank you Sir," she said, quickly pouring the coffee and reaching for the donut in the cupboard. He handed her the money and turned back to the table. None of the guys had come yet.

Placing the coffee silently before Mildred, he reclaimed his seat.

"What brings you here?" He asked without looking at her, stirring his thoroughly stirred coffee.

She took a bite of her donut and chewed it slowly. She seemed very hungry, and without looking at him, said quietly:

"I'm here, on a trade mission, with Gertrude. She is at the conference now, and rather than be alone at the hotel, she always leaves me alone, and having heard that you frequently come here, I decided to come and see you." She spoke hesitantly.

"Why?" he asked quietly, not looking at her.

"Seeking forgiveness?"

"For what? Why now?"

"Remembering what we had, I guess."

"To what purpose?"

"To put my soul at rest."

"You made your choice, so it should be at rest. Aren't you happy?"

There was a pause. He thought it was inordinately long, because the answer should have been spontaneous.

"Please don't torment me," she said.

She hadn't finished the donut. It was half-eaten on her napkin. He saw a shiver run through her.

"I have suffered my own torment for these many years. I have been to the brink. The only reason I am here is because the gods who govern my life decided that they did not want me yet. They sent me back." Harold said. "But I still want to know why."

He looked up instinctively and saw a tear coursing

down her cheek. He noticed that, unlike when they were together previously, she wore no makeup. Her skin was dry and her eyes were dull, not sparkling like before. There was a sadness in them.

"I made a mistake." she said. The tear fell on to the napkin she had crushed in her palm.

"Which mistake?"

"I actually made many mistakes."

She said it so softly he almost didn't recognise the words.

Harold looked at his watch. Time was passing quickly, although it seemed to be slow in passing. He waited for her to continue.

"I hurt you."

"Yes."

"I need to have reconciliation."

"Is that possible?'

"You tell me."

"No!! That's not possible at this time."

"Why not?" She looked at him, her eyes pleading.

"There is no need. That phase of our lives has passed under the bridge and gone downstream, even over the precipice. You made your decision like I did in the past, and we have to live with the results of those decisions."

"I know, but I thought..." There was pain in her voice, even hope.

"I'm sorry Mildred, but if you came thinking I would return to the past, you should know better. You have moved on in your life, and so have I."

He looked at his watch and, anxiously, at the entrance.

"I have built up new relationships. I was on the brink of death, and during my months of recovery from my Lymphoma, I have had time for retrospection and introspection. I understand your reasons for the decisions you made, and I have no intention of intruding into your life again.That phase is over."

"I am sorry..." she began.

"There can be no reconciliation," he continued. It was almost time for Sommers to arrive.

"When you read my memoirs you will understand."

She looked at the Movado watch. He looked at it also, and realised that it was one he had given her. It had been special.

"I'm sorry." she said. "I was hoping..." She gathered her bags and was preparing to leave.

Sommers arrived.

Harold looked at the set of her mouth that fury had reduced to slits on her face. Harold knew that the sight of Mildred was responsible for her anger.

When they discussed Mildred during their quiet times together and she got to know details of his earlier life, she always became angry and expressed it by the language she used.

"PM," she would say, "I can't stand the thought of what you went through at those times. If I ever meet up with her you can guess how I would behave."

She was always his defender.

She came up to him and kissed him without saying a word. She looked at Mildred. Wordlessly, she looked her up and down.

"I know who you are," she said slowly and quietly, but there was fury in the way she said it. "There is no need for my PM to introduce you. I am Sommers, and this gentleman is my man. From here on, I am warning you not to have anything to do with him. I know what you did to him, and I know what he went through. You are not good for him, and I will defend him from your kind. My advice to you is to leave and never have anything to do with him for the balance of his life."

Harold stood up. Sommers put herself between him and Mildred. Tears were running down Mildred's face. She looked at Harold and turned away. She was a beaten woman. She had lost her last gambit.

She walked out of the food court.

"Can I please have a cup of coffee, my love?" Sommers said quietly. It was as if the previous few minutes had never happened.

Harold walked quickly to the Tim Horton's counter and placed his order. The other members of the crew began to come one by one. He was glad they hadn't arrived sooner.

He brought the coffee over to Sommers and kissed her lightly on her cheek.

"My superwoman." he said in her ear.

She smiled.

Sommers became even more reclusive. She immersed herself more in her writing and preparation for her own presentation and defence of her thesis, while helping

Annie with her case.

Harold and Charlie were left very much to their own devices. But this burst of activity by the loves of their lives had an infectious effect, spurring them on to their own burst of activity.

Charlie had not only decided to return to studying, but he was busy preparing a project for the Seneca Nation, which had undertaken to build a number of bridges linking some of the islands in the Finger Lakes region. This would further his engineering experience and take him a step higher in his pursuit of a higher degree in Engineering.

Harold was more relaxed, and expected to be taking life more peacefully in the expectation that when Sommers graduated they would have a quiet life together.

They were now living together at Sommers' apartment, ever since Sommers had put her foot down and insisted that since she needed someone to scratch her back in places her hands could not reach, and since he was her chosen back scratcher, her chosen man, he was her designated personal back scratcher. In addition she let him know that if he did not move in with her she was going to stage a sit-in in the lobby of the apartment building he lived in."

He knew she meant it.

So he moved in with her, insisting that he would pay half of the rent. She agreed, but negotiated her way into buying groceries, sa;ying it was her duty to ensure that he ate proper food. He managed to convince her that he could cook just as well as she could, so they took turns at cooking and sharing house-hold duties. Life was good.

Harold and Sommers were seated in the living room when it arrived. Harold opened the door when the knock on it sounded, and he brought the envelope back to the settee.

"Look at this, Sommers," he said as they sat together on the settee. "This letter is from the Party back home. Hand delivered by courier. It must be important."

"Well, you won't know if you don't open it. Let's see what it is all about."

As he tore it open, she settled back into the comfortable position she had on his lap before the letter arrived. He was surprised at its contents when he read it aloud to her.

They wanted him back. They wanted him to contest the position of Party Leader again. He was assured of getting it, since the demand from the rank and file of the members was strong, and his experience was needed. Changes had taken place within the party structure, and a distinction had been made between the political leader concerned with the functioning of the Party in Parliament, and the Party leader concerned with he administration of the party itself.

A couple of his main nemeses had died. Others had left the Party for a higher calling—preaching—and some, like him, had left the island. The newer members who understood what had taken place were seeking his guidance.

"Do you want to go back?" she asked.

He didn't answer.

"If you want to, I will go back with you."

He still didn't answer. She wasn't deterred by his silence, for by now she understood that this silence was only an indication that his brain was, as he had said to her before, working in fifth gear and the engine was running at full speed.

She took the letter from his hand and read it through again.

"We can if you want to. I'm comfortable with whatever you decide. My studies are finished successfully, the graduation ceremony was great. Especially when they called me Dr. Blades—thanks to you—and I will soon be concentrating on my post-grad studies on the path you think I should take in looking at the question of reparations not only for African slaves, but also for indigenous Indians who were enslaved outside of this continent.

"This is an area where I will be collaborating with Annie. I am also considering researching the Gullah settlements and the history of those who, from the low country, were part of their history, their customs, and their African-ness, and the Barbadian connection, for their dialect and that of Barbadians are very close. That will keep me busy, and being a mother will keep me further occupied."

She sat upright and looked at him steadily, looking for his response and reaction to the hint she had subtly dropped.

It took him a little while, and then it hit him.

"What's that you said about being a mother?"

"I'm pregnant," she said quietly.

He stood up.

"Sommers, Sommers Blades, are you going to be a mother? Are you going to have a baby? Is this what you said?"

"Yes, I'm pregnant and I'm as happy as a woman can be, and more so because you are going to be the father."

He pulled her to him. As she looked into his eyes, water began to gather in hers also. Harold was crying. Although he hardly mentioned children in all the time they were together, he had told her of the son he had by Mildred, and how the loss affected him. Harold loved children. They seemed to mean a lot to him. Those little ones he came into contact with through his friends called him grandfather, and he accepted this moniker, even encouraged it with pride, and mentored those young people that he could.

She was happy she would be able to fill that void in his life that needed filling.

The phone was ringing insistently. It was late in the night and she really didn't want to be disturbed. It kept on ringing.

At last she answered sleepily. Harold was sleeping soundly. They were different—she heard the slightest sound, he needed to be shaken to wake him.

"Hello?"

'Hi Sommers." It was Annie.

"Sommers, it's Annie." She was excited, Sommers could hear it in her voice.

"I WON!!!" She had won her case. "We won!! In addition, I have great news for Charlie. I can't wait to tell him. I found out the background to Black Bear. I found out who Black Bear was and everything about him. There is a connection between him and Barbados, your country."

"What?! Annie are you sure?"

Sommers sat upright on the side of the bed. Harold reached across for her and then, realizing she was on the phone and sitting up, he sat up also.

"Who is it?" he asked.

"It's Annie. She won her case, and she also has news about Black Bear."

Harold was perplexed.

"Listen Annie," Sommers said, "let me know when you are returning and I will meet you at the airport. This news is too important to let you take it to the reservation before letting us know all the details. Instead of coming to Toronto come to Buffalo Airport, I will drive to the reservation, pick up Charlie, and we can all share this wonderful news back at the reservation where Charlie first told us about Black Bear."

"All right," Annie said. "I am so excited, I think I will have difficulty going to sleep. It's still early here, but I will listen to some classical music, some Chopin, that will calm me down. I'll let you know when I have made the arrangements for my flight. Nightie Night!" She hung up the phone.

CHAPTER 33

The Connection

The trip to the Seneca reservation was uneventful. Charlie was waiting for them, and he surprised them. He was wearing a business suit and looked completely different from when they had last seen him. He was very much the company executive, but his demeanour was that of a seemingly contented and serene personality. He was so much calmer, his brow was no longer furrowed and his well coifed hair and ruddy complexion were evidence of a healthy lifestyle. Sommers was really glad to see him. Harold gripped his hand tightly when they gave each other a friendly hug and shook hands.

He made Sommers stop at a flower shop to buy roses for Annie.

"I think she will like them," he said almost sheepishly. He seemed embarrassed to have this softer side of his personality exposed. "And they are to congratulate her on her success. She deserves them."

"I know she will be happy." Sommers said.

They were waiting at the entrance to the lobby when she

exited the plane. She was smiling broadly when she saw them, and when Charlie presented her with the roses her squeal of pleasure startled some of the passengers who were still coming off the plane. She rushed into Charlie's arms and kissed him long and hard.

"Charlie, thanks for being so thoughtful. I love you."

She hugged Sommers, and planted a kiss on Harold's cheek.

"Thanks for meeting me. I have so much news I can hardly wait to tell you about my trip, my case, my visit to the monuments, to the Trail of Tears, and how much I missed all of you, and most surprising and interesting of all was the information I found out about Black Bear. Let's hurry and get home."

"Alright," Sommers said. "We'll pick up something to eat on the way home, and eat there."

They left the airport. Sommers drove expertly and quickly, weaving in and out of the heavy traffic, and they were soon home.

Annie was in an expansive mood all the way home, but not so expansive that she did not have time to let Charlie know how much she missed him, how much she thought of him, and, to Sommers, how much she was in her thoughts, especially when she was able to use a lot of Sommers' research findings and knowledge of relationships and various cultures in her arguments before the court. At the end of her presentation, the justices concluded that failure to accept the legality of the marriage, and preventing the couple from exercising their constitutional rights to vote, could not be tolerated. Annie had won. She was highly commended by the justices on the merits of her presentation.

They were seated at the table in the kitchen of the bungalow. Annie was excited and pride of accomplishment showed in her attitude physically and emotionally.

"I was doubly excited the day the decision of the Supreme Court was handed down. The Justices gave their decision. It was unanimous.

She turned to Sommers.

"Their compliments were particularly pertinent, because of your input, especially with regard to relationships and customs between different ethnic groups.

"My most exciting news, however, concerns Black Bear. I took the opportunity to visit the memorial to the Trail of Tears. It was an epiphany for me. As I put a wreath on that memorial and quietly sat and cast my mind to what must have taken place on that migration, I felt the pain of those who were forced to make that genocidal journey. Knowing what I know about winter, my heart grieved at the thought of the suffering they must have undergone at that time, on that long march. I will always remember that feeling. I can never forgive the white man for what he did.

"While I was there I was fortunate to speak with a number of Cherokee who are descendants of those who were removed and travelled the trail, who were visiting the memorial. They told me the stories their parents and grandparents had told them about the trip from Georgia to Oklahoma. I mentioned what Charlie told us about the episode with Black Bear. Many of those with whom I spoke remember the episode, because his story, his bravery and kindness, lives on in Cherokee folklore. And Sommers, and PM, it seems that your country had a hand in it."

Sommers and Harold expressed surprise at this.

"Are you sure there is a connection with our country?" she asked.

"Absolutely." Annie answered.

"Black Bear was a Black-Cherokee. Apparently he was a slave in Barbados, who was sold to the neighbour of a Barbadian plantation owner named Drayton, who also owned a large plantation in Charleston called Drayton Hall. At his plantation and sugar mill and factory in Barbados, he had a slave named Ishi, who fathered a child, a girl child, from another slave. Drayton was so incensed when he found out about the child which he had hoped to father by the slave woman that he whipped Ishi and then sold him to Middleton who was a friend and one of the group of plantation owners who had settled Carolina. When Middleton came up to Carolina to visit his property, bringing some of his slaves with him, Ishi was among them.

"Some time after there was an Indian raid on the plantation, and some of the slaves, including Ishi, ran away. Ishi sought refuge among the Cherokees who sheltered him. He became assimilated, and became a member of the Cherokee tribes. They renamed him Black

Bear."

She turned to Charlie.

"Charlie," she said slowly, "Ishi, the slave from Barbados, was Black Bear. He was originally from Africa, was taken to Barbados and then arrived in Cherokee territory as a result of the raid at Middleton's plantation. Cherokee descendants still retell the history of Black Bear's exploits and how he gave his life to save the Cherokee lad who fell to his care following the death of his parents on the Trail of Tears. He walked the Trail of Tears also. He subsequently became a revered member of the tribe. Now you know Black Bear's background. I was so excited when I learned this story I could hardly wait to get back here to tell you about it."

Her audience were all silent and deeply contemplative for a long time when she finished.

Charlie broke the silence.

"Thank you Annie. I needed to hear this. I have often thought over the years about him. It was necessary to fill in this void in my background that was missing."

He reached across the table and kissed her.

"That is so interesting," Sommers added. "It just shows how intertwined human existence is. When backgrounds are traced, we find out that's why we need to be kinder and more loving to each other, because we never know how much closer we are in terms of relationships, more than we can even imagine."

The return to Scarborough was quiet. Conversation among them was sparse. The jazz music was soothing. There was a lot on their minds and conversation was not necessary. It was as if they could read each other's thoughts.

Harold reached across and held Sommers' hand.

"I love you beautiful lady," he said softly.

"I love you too, PM. Let's go back home."

"You are in control," he said. "At the rate you're driving it should take us only less than an hour to get there."

"I'm not talking about home now, silly," she said squeezing his fingers. "I'm talking about home to Barbados. I've been thinking a lot about the letter from the Party, my pregnancy and forcing myself to accept that I miss back there. I have spent a long time away, and I can do with the warmth of the climate, and the people that I have been close to. Besides, I miss Nicie."

"I've been thinking too," Harold said, "and now that I know you are going to be a mother I feel a greater need to be more protective."

"Yes, my dear," she said. She raised his hand to her lips and kissed it. "We have to make a number of plans about our future, so it will have to be carefully planned, especially with regard to the future of our child. I would like him, I know it will be a boy, to be born here. He was conceived here. It will take time to put everything in place, and by the time everything is over he will be ready to come into the world. I love Canada, and he should be part of it."

Sommers reached over in the bed for Harold. He wasn't there. She looked around for him, but only saw him when she went into the living room. He was sitting on the balcony, looking at the flow of traffic. It was going to be a lovely day, according to the weather report from the previous day. He had already made coffee, and was sitting, seemingly in deep thought, drinking slowly from the mug.

He became aware of her presence.

"The coffee is ready," he said without looking at her.

She tied the sash of her housecoat, poured a mug of coffee and without adding sugar or cream, cradled it in her hands and joined him.

"Sommers Blades," he said, looking at her directly. "Will you jump the broom with me?"

She was stunned.

"Well," he asked again, after what seemed to be a momentary hesitation, "will you marry me?"

"You can't spring that sort of question on a girl just like that. Especially so early in the morning. If you want to do that, or at least ask that sort of question, the setting has to be right... candlelight dinner, champagne, and so on. Not the first thing in the morning even before I get the sleep out of my eyes."

"Well," he said, "are you going to marry me or not? I already have the ring."

He pulled a small box from his pants pocket, and opened it showing her a beautiful solitaire diamond ring.

It sparkled in the early morning sunlight. She slowly put down the cup of coffee. Surprise was etched on her face. He took the ring and slipped it over her finger. It fit perfectly.

PM was always full of surprises. He went down on one knee. "Sommers Blades, are you going to agree to marry me or not? See I am down on my knee, and you better decide soon, I cannot stay long in this position."

"Of course I'll marry you PM. And stop trying to be so melodramatic. You know you didn't even have to ask."

"Good!" He said, slowly rising and resuming his seat.

She reached for him and kissed him deeply. "PM, I love you. Let's have some breakfast."

She nearly tripped over one of the other chairs because she was admiring the ring and not looking where she was going. She felt as if she would burst with excitement. She called Annie, she couldn't wait to break the news to her.

Annie was just as excited as Sommers when she told her of Harold's proposal, her acceptance, and about her plans for the return to Paradise and their future. She herself had exciting news also. She and Charlie were also planning to jump the broom in a couple of weeks. That set off another round of excitement and discussion of plans for their futures.

"Let's plan to do that in Barbados. Come down with us, or meet us there. What do you think of that?" Sommers suggested to her.

"That would be great," Annie answered. "We need to get away for some time in another place where we can relax, away from the hectic atmosphere we presently live in here. I'll put this to Charlie and get back to you. Although I am sure he will agree. It would be good for us to see this place that has produced people like you and PM. Let's get together very soon. By the way I got a promotion at the law firm. I have been recommended for a partnership, if I want it."

More excitement.

"Alright," Sommers said in agreement. She was sure Harold would have no objection. They had discussed their plans for resettling in Barbados. His bungalow had been taken care of by a caretaker during the time he was away. It would easily suit their purposes. It was large enough, and the atmosphere was peaceful enough to provide the healing necessary for recuperation. It was really a paradise to which they could return."

Paradise occupied their thoughts when she sat and discussed the proposals with Harold.

"It has been an interesting journey," he said, "and the future looks bright for all of us. However, even though my future within the party looks promising, I plan to just assist them in winning the next election, but I will resist all attempts to make me political leader and try to get elected to Parliament. I will accept the position of Party Leader, but I will ensure that I put you and my baby first of all. Thank you Dr. Blades, for making my life complete. Thank you Sommers."

They held hands and watched the changing colours the setting sun painted on the canvas of the evening sky.

When Annie and Charlie came down to Scarborough the following week, Sommers and Annie ignored the two men. They were too busy discussing 'woman things' as Sommers said. But Harold and Charlie were busy with their own plans, and their own surprises, especially Charlie, who revealed his pleasure at being invited to visit Barbados, especially now that it had special relevance for him. He wanted to learn everything he could about the country, and Harold gave him all the information he wanted.

They looked forward to the future with expectations great.

CHAPTER 34

Home

It was just after midnight when the pains began. It was time.

She had prepared for some time before; actually Harold had prepared. For weeks he had been visiting stores examining and checking baby clothes and everything connected with the anticipated birth of their son. He had accompanied her on every visit to the doctor, had closely examined the images of her ultrasound tests, even more closely than she did. He was excited at the pending birth.

She woke him.

"Its time, my love."

By the time she had readied herself, he had the car warmed up—it was still very cool even though it was spring—and had put her suitcase in the car. He was waiting to help her into the vehicle as she came to the door. He drove very carefully to the hospital, where the nurses were waiting for them when they arrived.

He was in the surgical gown, scrubbed and waiting at the door of the delivery room when she was wheeled inside. He was going to be with her during the entire delivery process. He had conceived his son, and intended to be there to bring him into the world. Although she was slightly groggy from the medication, she smiled at his presence and was glad when he sat at the head of the bed to comfort her. She reached out and gently touched his hand, especially when a contraction engulfed her in pain soon after she was settled on the bed.

She gripped his hands tightly when the next one came, and would have laughed when he began deep breathing with her between the contractions, if she could have.

She was too busy bringing her baby into the world.

He was born soon after, without any complications. The tall obstetrician from the West Indies was quietly efficient, and his competent staff made her birthing easier.

One nurse wiped the perspiration from his forehead as the other one placed their son on Sommers breast, between them.

Harold kissed her, and the baby.

"Thank you," he said to her.

He felt heady as he inhaled the odour of his newborn son.

Annie and Charlie were at the hospital early the next morning. He had phoned Charlie soon after he left the delivery room.

"Charlie. We have a son."

"Congratulations," Charlie said. "We will be there early tomorrow."

They came as promised.

It was early morning. He was standing on the balcony of the apartment. He was speaking to his son in his arms, but she couldn't understand what he was saying. She pulled her house coat closer around her body.

"It's cool out here you know," she said to him. "Don't you think it is too early for him to be outside?"

She reached into his arm and kissed the baby, who was sleeping peacefully, seemingly enjoying the warmth of his father's body.

"I have been thinking," he said gently. "It's time to go back home."

"Whenever you're ready," she replied, hugging him. "I was only waiting for you to mention it. It's time for him to be welcomed to his other home."

"We have to finalize arrangements and coordinate with Annie and Charlie. Remember they promised to go with us," she said.

"Yes," he said. "I'll, call Charlie and we'll start making preparations. Annie has already obtained their passports and already informed the members of the firm that she may be leaving for a vacation, so it won't be too difficult for her. Besides, they owe her time off for her performance at the Oklahoma trial."

He carefully placed the baby in the crib in their bedroom, seemingly reluctant to leave it. He had been this way, from the time he first brought it home.

In just a few weeks they were ready to leave for Barbados.

In the five-hour flight home, the baby, remarkably, only cried briefly a few hours after they were in the air, and after Sommers fed him he fell asleep once more and was this way for the rest of the flight, stirring slightly when the bump of the landing wheels indicated that they were home.

The sun was already high in the blue sky when they came out onto the balcony of the bungalow. It was a bright sunny day. The breeze was blowing steady over the waves coming in to the shore. The sound of children in the nearby school singing attracted Charlie's notice. He cocked his head to one side to better hear the words.

"Onward and upward we shall go, inspired, exalted, free..."

"Those are the words of our National Anthem," Harold said quietly, with pride. "They sing the anthem at schools every day. We are proud of our small nation, and positive reinforcement of our values is necessary to maintain that drive for excellence."

Annie was very thoughtful as she looked over the East coast.

"We have a beautiful country," she said.

There seemed to be contentment and sincerity in her pronouncement.

Harold was happy to be back home. Old places began to

seem familiar again. With the passage of time more of his friends, those he could remember—many had passed on—and some had to be researched a long time in his memory banks.

His sister Kimberley was happy to see him, to meet his new family and her new relatives, her new nephew, and anxious to be brought up to date with his experiences while they were apart.

When she spoke with Sommers she expressed surprise at her background.

"Harold," she said, "do you know that we have Scottish blood in our background, like Sommers' relatives?"

"Can't be true." Harold answered. "Where did you get that idea?"

"Well, since you went away I have been curious about our background. Adriana, my niece, has a daughter that strike back."

"What do you mean strike back?" Harold answered. He was puzzled.

"Well, as you know she has three children. One of them, the girl, when she was an infant began to develop reddish hair. Adriana's husband is dark, like her, and everybody was puzzled that she was a lighter complexion than her brothers, and that she had a bone structure that was not like the rest of the family. As she grew I began to think back on our family, and realised that she was growing more and more like one of our aunts. She was big boned and lighter in complexion, and had facial and other features just like some of the red-legs of St.

John."

"This is very interesting," Harold said. "I have not seen any of them since they were born."

"More than that," Kimberley said, "our family history goes back to Scotland. Our grandmother on our father's side goes back as far as Robert the Bruce, a very famous highlander. We have Scottish ancestors on one side, and on our father's side we have relations deriving from the Spanish side of Panama. Our grandfather worked on the Panama Canal. He was one of the silver men. Our mother grew up in the Canal Zone of the Panama Canal. She went to school in the Canal Zone."

"I know about that part," Harold said, "because she told me about it when I was very young. But I never delved into our ancestry."

"Well, I tried to trace it," Kimberley said. "I learned that our great grandmother was Spanish. Her family name was Capitano, but I have never had the time to go further back in the archives. Maybe now you are back home we can work together on getting our ancestry settled and our family tree, and its roots firmly established."

"Based on what you say, I think we have a big job before us for it looks like our friends may turn out to be more closely related than any of us realise."

"PM," Sommers said looking steadfastly at her sister in law, "this issue of our friends and relations seems more intertwined and involved than any of us have ever imagined. We have a lot of work before us. Since we know that Cherokees were enslaved and sent to Barbados, we may even find out that Charlie may have relatives still descended from his ancestors. He may even find out that Ishi's relations are still here."

"We have work to do," she answered.

Postscript

There is no difference

Within the pages of *Friends and Relations*, reference is made to the writing of Allan Gallay: the Warner R. Woodring Chair of Atlantic World and Early American History at Ohio State University, where he is Director of the Center for Historical Research. His observations and discussion on Indian Slavery in the Americas are quoted in this novel. He points out that: "...the story of European colonialism in the Americas and its victimization of Africans and Indians follows a central paradigm in most textbooks.

"The African role encompasses the transportation, exploitation, and suffering of many millions in New World slavery, while Indians are described in terms of their succumbing in large numbers to disease, with the survivors facing dispossession of their land. This paradigm—a basic one in the history of colonialism—omits a crucial aspect of the story: the indigenous peoples of the Americas were enslaved in large numbers. This exclusion distorts not only what happened to American

Indians under colonialism, but also points to the need for re-assessment of the foundation and nature of European overseas expansion."

Gallay, in his pamphlet, includes a number of photographs of indigenous Indians, from Tainos to Piegan (Blackfoot: Pikani) from the Northern Great Plains, who inhabited lands in Montana and in Alberta, Canada. These are reproduced here to give readers a better perspective and understanding of who these indigenous Indians were. The visual presentation allows the reader a better understanding of what these people looked like. They see children, young people and adults, and are better able to differentiate between the 'picture' presented by Hollywood—whites cosmetically made into Indians—and Blacks in caricature, and photographs which show them as they are.

He makes no mention of the colour of the peoples who were the inhabitants of this huge continent. The notable characteristic of which is that they were Black.

I would posit that the reality of the European colonization of the Americas is that when the Europeans first discovered that this land was occupied by Blacks who owned it, their innate prejudices, evidenced by their earlier encounters with Blacks in and from Africa, made them unable to accept that this land was not theirs, but belonged to Black people. They would thus have to deal with these people, and their desires differently.

I would also posit that this precipitated the long term objective of taking this land away from its inhabitants by any means necessary, including enslavement, force of arms, wars and genocide. This is stated in their enunciated Doctrine of Manifest Destiny. These people were 'savages'—like the people in Africa—and needed to be 'civilized' and it was their destiny to do this in exchange for which the land was destined for them "to the exclusion of all others.

There is no difference between the African from whichever part of that vast continent, and the Apache, or Choctaw, the Seminole from Florida or the Ibo from Nigeria. Hollywood and propaganda have perpetuated the myth, and have fostered the belief that there is a difference between indigenous Indians and African Blacks, and thus infer different kinds of enslavement: "Blacks were more suited to enslavement in America because Indians were difficult to keep enslaved because of their penchant to run away."

There is no difference, and the rebellions, wars, uprisings, escapes, and general insurrection, when they were undertaken by Blacks and indigenous Indians in the Americas when they were enslaved there, or in the West Indies when Indians were enslaved and shipped from their homes in America to plantations in Antigua, Barbados, Martinique or wherever. This is proof positive that the excuses given for enslavement are spurious and in need of condemnation and remembrance.

"Indian slavery was a central means by which early colonists funded economic expansion. In the late seventeenth and early eighteenth centuries, a frenzy of enslaving occurred in what is now the eastern United States. English and allied Indian raiders nearly depopulated Florida of its American Indian population. From 1670 to 1720 more Indians were shipped out of Charleston, South Carolina than Africans were imported as slaves, and Charleston was a major port for bringing in Africans."

There is no difference between indigenous Indian enslavement and African (imported) slavery (enslavement) in the Americas. No difference between the indigenous Indian enslaved to silver mine owners in Central America, and African slaves working on sugar plantations in Barbados; between Blacks working on cotton plantations in Virginia, Alabama, or South Carolina and the Choctaw or Apache, shipped to work in Martinique. There is no difference between the Irish man captured in England and exported as a slave to Barbados, or the Taino, captured by Columbus and shipped to Queen Isabella to be sold on the auction block in Lisbon.

There is no difference between the slave trader in Georgia yesterday, and the slaveholder in Tripoli today, selling refugees from Libya or other places in Africa, fleeing against economic conditions and sold to buyers with the same attitudes and motivations of traders of centuries past.

There is no difference.

Sources Cited

1. *The Slave History of Barbados: Settlement, Plantocracy, Rebellion and Emancipation.* http://funbarbados.com//ourisland/history.
2. Miles, Tiya. *Pain of Trail of Tears. Shared by Blacks as well as Native Americans.*
3. *Carolina: The African Slaves.* http:www.Carolin.com/Carolina/Settlement/ African slaves in carolina.html.
4. *The Sad History of the 'Redlegs' of Barbados.* http://planetbarbadosblog.com/2009/05/ giving-voice-to-theredlegs-of Barbados. accessed21/06/2017
5. Stuart, Andrea. *Sugar in the Blood: A Family's Story of Slavery and Empire.* Review. Accessed 21/06/2017
6. *Indian Removal and the Trail of Tears.* https://thoughtsco.com/the-trail-of-tears-1773597. accessed 20/6/2017
7. *Ten Things to Know About Andrew Jackson* https://www.bbc.co.uk/british/emireseapower/ barbados 01.shtml
8. *Slavery and Economy in Barbados.* By Dr. Karl Watson seapower/barbados01.shtml
9. *Caribbean Project: Colonizing the North American*

Mainland. Hunter Wallace project-colonizing north america/19/05/21017

10. *Retracing Slavery's Trail of Tears.* http:www.tears180956968. Accessed26/04/2017

11. Caribbean Project: The Barbados-South Carolina Connection-Occidental dissent.com/2014/02/15/ caribbean-project-thebarbados-couth-carolina...

12. Onion, Rebecca. *America's Other Original Sin.* http:slate.com/articles/news

13. *The Irish Slave Trade-The Forgotten 'White Slaves': The Slaves Time Forgot.* By John Martin. http:www.globalsearch.ca/the-irish-slave-trade-theforgotten-white-slaves/31076. Accessed 10/05/2017

14. *White Women and Slavery in the Caribbean.* Hilary McD Beckles. https://www.jetor.org/ stable/4289252?seq=3

15. *A Short History of the Slave Trade* https://www.thoughtco.com/African-slavery-101-44535 accessed 19/05/2017

16. Gillo-Whittaker, Dino. *The Untold History of American Slavery.* https://www.thoughtsco.com/ untold-history-of-americans-indian-slavery

17. *Carolina-The Barbadian Influence. How did Barbados and its Short History 'Influence' Carolina* influences/Barbadians_in_Carolina_html. accessed 19/05/2017

18. Willard, Fred. *The Machapungo Indians and the Barbados Connection: 1663-1840.* East Carolina

University.

19. Brewer Stewart, James. *Holy Warriors:The Abololitionis and American Slavery.* American Century Series. A division of Farrar, Straus and Giroux. McGraw Hill Ryerson Ltd. Toronto.

20. Neal Minges, Patrick. *All My Slaves, Whether Negroes Indians, Mustees. Toward a Thick Description of Slave Religion.* http://are.wva/ minges.htm accessed 05/09/2017

21. *Contrasting Beginnings of Slavery in North America* http://idhi.library .cofe.edu.exhibits/show/ africanpassagesloecountryadapt/section_intro 07/09/2017

22. Krauthamer, Barbara. *Black Slaves, Indian Masters:Slavery,Emancipation and Citizenship in the Native American South* (2013)-emancipation-and-citizenship....accessed 25/08/2017

23. Jennings, Julianne. *The Tragic History of African Slaves and Indians.* https:// Indiancountrymedianetwork.com/news/opinions/ the-tragic-history-of-african-slave. Accessed 25/08/2017

24. Wilcox, P.J. *The Unknown Native American/ Amerindian Slave Trade.* http://www.linkedin. com/pulse/unknown-native-americanamerindian-slave-trade-pj-wilc...

25. *English Trade in Deerskins and Indian Slaves.* Robbie Etheridge, University of Mississippi. New Georgia Encylopedia. 30/8/2017

26. Resendez, Andres. *The Other Slavery. The Uncovered Story of Indian Enslavement in America.*

27. *The Religious Origins of Manifest Destiny.* html file The Religious Origins of Manifest Destiny. Divining America. Accessed 2/4/2016

28. Mulraine, Lloyd E. *Barbadian Americans-History, Modern era. The First Barbadians in America.* American.html

29. *African-Native.Americans: We are still here: a Photo Exhibit.* http://www.barach.C.U.N.Y.edu/library. alumni/online_exhibits/digital/native/native_ thumbs.

30. Corrie, Damon. *The Unknown Native American/ Amerindian Slave Trade and the Barbados and Guyana Lokono-Arawak Origins of the Infamous Salem Witch Trials.*

31. Cummins, Alvin. *JaJa King of Opobo. A Play in Two Acts.* (Caribbean Chapters)

32. *Slavery and Involuntary Servitude.* http://what-when-how.com/sociology/slavery and involuntary-servitude.

33. Watson, Dr. Karl. *British History in Depth:Slavery and Economy in Barbados.* empire_seapower/

34. Calloway, Dane. *New DNA Proves African Americans Are In Fact Indigenous Aborigines of America.* https://justheretomakeyouthink (2016-2021)

35. Grant, R.G. *Slavery: Real people and their stories of Enslavement.* Dorling Kindersley Limited. London

36. Grann, David. *Killers of the Flower Moon. The Osage Murders and the Birth of the FBI.*

37. OuterBridge Packwood, Cyril. *Chained On The Rock. Slavery in Bermuda.* Edited by C.F.E. Hollis Hallett. Second Edition 2012 National Museum of Bermuda Press

38. Calloway, Dane. *New DNA proves African Americans Are In Fact Indigenous Aborigines of America* 2016/12/fb_img_1481447304254.jpg

39. Lowcountry Digital History Initiative. *Barbadians in Carolina.* http://Idhi.library.cofc.edu/exhibits/show/africanpassagesslowcountryadapt/sectionii_intro

About Alvin Cummins

"Cummins' forte lies in his ability to create wonderfully real characters whom he breathes life into until their presence brings each page alive with warmth, compassion and pathos."

Wayne Jordan (Author)

Alvin Cummins was born in Barbados in 1933 and attended Combermere Boys' School. He left the island in 1958 to attend Harper College, of the State University of New York (SUNY) on a tuition waiver, where he studied for the Bachelor's Degree, with a major in Biology. Upon completion trained as a Medical Technologist, and became a Fellow of the Society of Medical Technologists of the West Indies. He returned to Barbados in 1963 and assumed the position of Senior Technologist at the Queen

301

Elizabeth Hospital. The desire for further study resulted in training at the College of Physicians and Surgeons of Columbia University in New York and a certificate in Exfoliative Cytology, and after a journey to the University of the West Indies; Mona campus where he completed his BSc (Special) in Clinical Microbiology and a MSc. in Microbiology.

It was in Jamaica in 1970 that he commenced work on his first novel: "The Wind Also Listens," a novel that traces a young Barbadian's "escape" from the stultifying and prejudiced-filled atmosphere that was pre-independence Barbados. It also highlights the ways in which other young people 'escaped' from that society, migrating to other countries to seek better lives. He migrated to Toronto, Canada, the same year, resulting in a halt to the book's completion until 1997. In Toronto he worked at Mt. Sinai Hospital, as Charge Technologist in the Microbiology Department. His first Scientific Publication, appeared in the Journal of Clinical Microbiology in 1973. At the same time he completed studies at the University of Toronto, obtaining a Diploma in Public Administration, and also obtained a Diploma in Hospital and Health Care Administration, from the University of Saskatchewan

After resigning from Mt. Sinai in 1980, he was appointed as Supervisor of Microbiology, from 1981 to 1983, at Hamad Hospital, in Doha, Qatar. He returned to Barbados in 1985 and established Med-Chem Laboratories, a private medical diagnostic laboratory, and commenced research on "Azole Antifungal Resistance in Vaginal

Candidiasis," at the University of the West Indies; Cave Hill Campus, reading toward his Ph.D in Microbiology, and was awarded the M.Phil degree in 2007.

His contribution to the Literary Arts include four plays, three musicals (book and lyrics), three novels; with another one completed but not yet published. Two of the novels, *The Royal Palms are Dying* and *The Wind Also Listens*, were joint winners of the Prime Minister's Award at the Frank Collymore Literary awards (2007), while a play, *The Home Coming,* received literary awards at the National Independence Festival of Creative Arts (NIFCA).

He has been an actor, a member of the Green Room Players, performing from Shakespeare to a Barbadian adaptation of Broadway's *Fiddler on the Roof* (Okras in the Stew). He has performed in Television plays: *Domino Alley*, radio dramas: *The Brathwaites of Black Rock*, and *Dot and Dash*, and the recently released movie *Sweet Bottom.*

Friends and Relations is his most recent addition to the literary pantheon of Barbados.

Addendum

When I first suggested to a friend what I had posited in my 'Postscript' to this book, (he used to teach History to Secondary school students) his reaction was scepticism and even ridicule: "if you say these things people will laugh at you," and I wondered briefly whether I should abandon my ideas. In defence, I decided to copy some of my references and include them in this Addendum; especially the coloured reproductions of photographs of some of the subjects, to justify their inclusion.

I consider these truths important for a better understanding of the psychological impact of the events of the past on our reactions today. Full recognition is given to the original articles and the authors, with no intention of seeking to benefit from their scholarship.

The truth must, however, be told and reinforced. It is hoped that others will pursue greater in depth study and documentation of these important pages of our history.

> "Many of these early slaves were American Indians, mostly Algonquian-speakers of coastal Virginia and North Carolina. By the 1680s, English settlers routinely kidnapped Native American women and children in the coastal plains of North Carolina and Virginia. This Native American slave trade involved

a number of colonies, including Virginia, Carolina, Pennsylvania, Massachusetts, Jamaica, Barbados, St. Kitts, and Nevis. So many Indian slaves were traded to Pennsylvania that a law was passed in 1705 forbidding the importation of Carolina Indian slaves. This was done in part because many of the slaves were Tuscarora who were aligned militarily with the Iroquois Confederacy, which threatened to intervene to stop the trade.

"From 1680 to 1715, the English sold thousands of Indians into slavery, some as far away as the Caribbean. Indian slavery, however, had many problems, not the least of which were Indian attacks, and by 1720, most colonies in North America had abandoned it for African slavery. In 1670, Virginia passed a law defining slavery as a lifelong inheritable "racial" status. After the passage of this law many "black Indians" found themselves classified as black and forced into slavery.

"In the fields and homes of colonial plantations, mutually enslaved African Americans and American Indians forged their first intimate relations. In spite of a later tendency in the Southern colonies to differentiate the African slave from the Indian, chattel slavery was built on a preexisting system of Indian slavery. Even though the arrival of Africans in 1619 began to change the face of slavery in North America from "tawny" Indian to "blackamoor" African, Indian slaves were exported throughout the Caribbean often in trade for Africans. As the 18th century dawned the slave trade in American Indians was so serious that it eclipsed the trade for furs and skins and had become the primary source of commerce between the English and the South Carolina colonials (Minges 2002:454).

"During this transitional period, Africans and Americans Indians shared the common experience of enslavement. They worked together, lived together in communal quarters, produced collective recipes for food, shared herbal remedies, myths and legends and in the end they intermarried. Africans had a disproportionate numbers of males in their population while Native American women and children were disproportionately enslaved. American Indians males were shipped to the Caribbean, died in wars or of European diseases. As traditional societies in the Southeast were primarily matrilineal, African males who married American Indians women often became members of the wife's clan and of her nation

"The 1740 slave codes of South Carolina served to blur the distinction between African, American Indian and the children of their intermarriage, declaring: All negroes and Indians, (free Indians in amity with this government, and negroes, mulattoes, and mustezoses, who are now free, excepted) mullatoes and mustezoes who are now, or shall hereafter be in this province, and all their issue and offspring...shall be and they are hereby declared to be, and remain hereafter absolute slaves (Hurd 1862:303 as cited in Minges 2002:455)"

https://www.nps.gov/ethnography/aah/aaheritage/lowCountry_furthRdg1.htm

Mescalero Apaches (along with US representatives)

Medicine Pipe and Fool Dog, 1873. Arapaho tribe

Chief Spotted Elk of the Mniconjou tribe, aka Big Foot

Sioux chief Crazy Horse

Sioux chief Sitting Bull

Oglala chief Red Cloud

Old Crow and wife Pretty Medicine Pipe, 1873. Crow tribe

Iron Bull and wife, 1873. Crow tribe

Drayton Hall, South Carolina